Also by Onjali Q. Raúf

The Boy at the Back of the Class

The Star Outside My Window

THE NIGHT BUS

Hero

ONJALI Q. RAÚF

DELACORTE PRESS

Text copyright © 2020 by Onjali Q. Raúf
Map copyright © 2020 by Pippa Curnick
Jacket art copyright © 2020 by Pippa Curnick

Visit us on the Web! rhcbooks.com

Educators and librarians, for a variety of teaching tools, visit us at RHTeachersLibrarians.com

Library of Congress Cataloging-in-Publication Data is available upon request.
ISBN 978-0-593-38202-8 (hc)—ISBN 978-0-593-38204-2 (lib. bdg.)—
ISBN 978-0-593-38205-9 (ebook)

The text of this book is set in 11.5-point Warnock Pro Light.
Interior design by Cathy Bobak

Printed in the United States of America
10 9 8 7 6 5 4 3 2 1
First U.S. Edition

Dedicated to the real Thomas—a man I never had the courage to know—and everyone being forced to sleep rough on our world's streets.

And for Mum and Zak. Always.

Perhaps one did not want to be loved so much
as to be understood.
—George Orwell

To make a home for the homeless . . . whatever
the world may say, it cannot be wrong.
—Vincent van Gogh

Contents

Two Snakes and the School Soup

"HECTOOOOOOOOORRRRRRRGGGGGH! STOP RIGHT THERE!"

I froze with my hand hovering above the large vat of bright red tomato soup. It would have been a perfectly ordinary pot of soup, if it hadn't been for the long, bright green rubber snake that was now floating around right in the middle of it.

"HECTOOOOORRR! I'M WARNING YOU!"

I slowly turned to look over my shoulder. I could see all the lunch ladies in their bright blue uniforms staring at me with their mouths wide open, like doors someone had forgot to shut. Everyone in the cafeteria had frozen. Except for Mr. Lancaster. His mouth was open wide too and getting wider like a big black hole. I could tell he was getting ready to explode, because his face had gone as pink as a baboon's bottom and his nose was starting to twitch.

"Don't you dare," he hissed, glaring at the second rubber snake I was holding in my hand.

1

I looked down at the second snake. This one was bright red. Almost as bright red as the boring soup Mrs. Baxter had made.

I knew I had two options. The first one was to *not* drop the second snake in. I would still get punished for the green snake, but maybe it wouldn't be quite as bad.

The second option was to drop the snake in. That would make Mr. Lancaster even madder than he already was and make Mrs. Baxter *really* mad. But it would serve her right for being the worst lunch lady we'd ever had—always narrowing her eyes and giving us the smallest spoonfuls of the things we wanted, and plonking giant spoonfuls of the things we hated onto our plates. It was about time someone got her back. Plus it would make Will and Katie, my two best friends, laugh.

"WELL? *WELL?*" said Mr. Lancaster.

Looking back at Mr. Lancaster, I grinned and let go of the snake. A gasp echoed around the cafeteria as the second rubber snake joined the first with a splash. Blobs of tomato soup flew out everywhere. A splodge landed with a *SPLAT* on Mrs. Baxter's head. A second lump hit with a *SCHLOP* on another lunch lady's cheek. A third struck with a *GLOOP* on Mr. Lancaster's twitchy nose and oozed down to the floor with a *drip, drip, drip.*

"RIGHT, YOUNG MAN! YOU'VE DONE IT NOW! COME WITH ME!"

That's a thing people call me when they get really angry—"young man." It's as if they're so mad they can't remember my name. In fact, no one ever says my name normally anymore. It's either "young man" or "HECTOOOOOOOORRRR" shouted in a voice that tells me right away that the person is angry with me. Even Will and Katie just call me "H." But I don't care. I used to, but I don't anymore. Most people are so stupid that it doesn't matter what they think of me. They're like those tiny annoying flies that buzz around you when you're trying to eat ice cream. The worst part is, the stupidest, most annoying bugs in the country all seem to be at my school.

I imagined what it might be like to swat people with a giant fly swatter, as Mr. Lancaster started to march me out of the cafeteria. I gave Will and Katie a wink on my way out—after all, I had won our bet! But they were laughing so hard I don't think they even saw me.

"SIT RIGHT THERE AND DON'T YOU DARE SAY A WORD!" snapped Mr. Lancaster, pointing at the detention sofa.

Mr. Lancaster is the principal, and sometimes I wonder if the certificates on his wall are really secret awards given to him for being the stupidest and most annoying principal in the country. The funny thing is, he *thinks* he's clever. He's always watching me and waiting to catch me out just so that he can cry "HECTOOOOOORRRRR!" in front of the whole school. When he does that, the veins in his neck go from being two-dimensional to three-dimensional. He's always giving me weird warnings too. Last week it was: "ONE more time and you'll be out on your ears so quick, your head will be spinning like the solar system!"

Today it's: "You're THIS close to getting your legs chopped right off from under you, young man! And then what will you be? Legless! That's what!"

If Mr. Lancaster really wants to get rid of me or my legs, he'll have to do a better job of catching me. He got lucky today 'cos I guess he must have been spying on me extra hard. But he doesn't know the half of what I get up to, because I can see his stupid traps from miles away. Like the time he installed tiny cameras that looked like shiny black beetles outside the boys' bathroom; he was hoping to catch me taking payment from those who *didn't* want their hair washed in the toilets at lunchtime. But of course, I saw the cameras right away. Now I wave to them every day as I walk past, before taking all my payments in the far corner of the playground. It works out well for everyone. No one gets a toilet dunking, and I get a steady supply of other people's pocket money and sweets.

Then there was the time last year when Mr. Lancaster made all the school prefects into lunch monitors and gave them huge shiny badges. Their job was to try and stop me from tripping people up when they were carrying their lunch trays to their tables. But I just tripped the lunch monitors up instead, and they all quit the very next day.

"HECTOOORRR! ARE YOU LISTENING?!" Mr. Lancaster's angry voice interrupted my happy memory of tripping up Katie Lang and watching her tumble head over heels across the cafeteria while her bowl of chili splattered half of her schoolmates. "YOU HAD BETTER NOT EVEN *THINK* ABOUT MISSING DETENTION TODAY!"

Before Mr. Lancaster could continue, the school bell began to ring as if it had also had enough of him. Trying not to grin, I nodded and slowly—very, very slowly—made my way back to my classroom. By the time I reached it, everyone was already inside getting out their workbooks.

"Hectorrrr!" sighed Mrs. Vergara, picking up the class roster again and shaking her head. "Why must you ALWAYS be late?" she asked, scratching her head now too.

I shrugged and slumped down into my chair next to Rajesh. Mrs. Vergara is *always* shaking and scratching her head at me. It's as if she secretly has lice and only remembers that they itch whenever I'm in the room.

"OK, OK. Settle down," she said, walking over to the whiteboard with a bright green marker in her hand. "Now that everyone is *finally* here, let's recap the events leading up to the Great Fire of London."

I realized my workbook was in my drawer at the front of the classroom and gave a silent groan. Not that I cared really. I sat and watched as Mrs. Vergara's pen made big, loopy letters on the board, leaving behind a shiny green trail just like a slug's.

"Pssssssst! Rajesh!" whispered a boy's voice from the table in front of us, where Robert and Mei-Li sat. A small piece of folded paper landed near my elbow.

Before Rajesh could reach for it, I grabbed the note and opened it up. It was a funny drawing of Mrs. Vergara with flames coming out of her bum as if her farts had caught on fire. The words "How the Great Fire of London REALLY started" were written above it. I looked over at Robert, impressed. I didn't think that a brainiac like him would have the guts to draw something so funny about a teacher. Usually any bits of paper he passed to Rajesh had math equations on them or said something like "Meet me in the library by the chemistry section." But then, from over his shoulder, I saw Karina looking nervously at me. It was obviously her drawing that Robert had been passing along.

"Hectorrrrrrrrrrrrrrrr. Something keeping you busy, is it?"

I quickly scrunched the paper up in my hands. But it was too late. Mrs. Vergara was already standing in front of me.

"Give it here. *Now*," she said softly, her head tilting to one side.

I looked over at Rajesh, whose eyes were popping so far out of his head they looked like they were going to fly across the room, and then glanced at Mei-Li and stupid Robert. Mei-Li was frowning at Robert, and Robert was sitting up straight and looking at the ceiling as if he had never seen it before. I could see Karina doing the same thing too. Giving them all a scowl, I handed the drawing over to Mrs. Vergara.

I knew exactly what she was going to do next, because unfortunately, Mr. Lancaster isn't the only champion-level stupid person at my school. Mrs. Vergara is just as stupid, except instead of trying to catch me at things, she pretends to be nice to me. That's one of the tricks extra-sneaky grown-ups like to use when they want you to think they're your friend and not your enemy.

Looking down at the drawing, Mrs. Vergara shook her head. Again. "Oh, Hectoooooorrrr! I'm disappointed in you. I know you're so much better than this."

"But—but it wasn't me! It was Karina's! She passed it to Mei-Li, and Robert to give to Rajesh!"

Karina gasped, and Robert shook his head. Mei-Li opened her mouth, but before she could say anything, Mrs. Vergara bent down and pointed one long finger at me.

"DON'T blame *them* for YOUR behavior," said Mrs. Vergara. "This drawing is insulting and rude enough without you lying too. I just wish you could trust me enough to tell me the truth. I'm afraid I'll have to give you detention AGAIN."

I opened my mouth to argue that it really hadn't been me—and that if it had, my drawing would have been *way* better and funnier—but I knew there wasn't any point. Whenever a grown-up tells me to trust them, I know it's the last thing I can do. Grown-ups only ever help people they like, and I've never met a single grown-up who likes me. Besides, I've been disappointing everyone since as far back as I can remember, so that wasn't anything new.

Mrs. Vergara walked back to the whiteboard and asked a question about the fire. I saw Mei-Li looking at me, so I gave her a scowl, which made her turn away. As bad as Mr. Lancaster and Mrs. Vergara are, there's nothing worse than brainiacs and teacher's pets, which is exactly what Mei-Li and Robert are. The boys are always called "brainiacs," and the girls are always called "teacher's pets," but they're both just as annoying as each other.

You can always tell right away if someone's a brainiac or a teacher's pet, because they act like it's the end of the world if they don't get an A or a gold star on all their tests. They NEVER forget their homework. In fact, some of them are so disgusting they even do *extra* homework. And all of them suck up to the teachers so much that their lips get stuck in a pout. Just go and see. Go and find a brainiac or a teacher's pet, and you'll see their lips are redder and poutier than everyone else's. Sadly, you probably won't have to look far, because every class in every school on the whole planet has got at least one. But I guess my class is the unluckiest class in the world, because we've got three. *Three* horrible sucker-uppers in one classroom. It's a nightmare.

There's Nathasha, who sits right next to Mrs. Vergara's desk and jumps up and down on her chair like a giant frog whenever she knows the answer to something. Then there's Robert, who thinks he's funny as well as clever even though he isn't either. They're both too scared to even look at me most of the time, so they like to pretend I don't exist. But *the* worst, *the* most irritating and *the* most pet-like pet of all the teacher's pets in all the world is definitely Mei-Li.

She joined our class last year, and even though she doesn't speak like the rest of us and brings smelly foods for lunch like bright orange noodles and weird balls wrapped in black plastic, all the teachers love her. She has shiny black hair that's always in a ponytail, which she flicks whenever she gets something right, and she's always chewing on the end of a pencil, which makes her look just like a giraffe eating straw. She never gets anything less than ninety percent on every single test, and she holds the record for having the most awards for anything that my stupid school gives awards for, even though she's so new. She would probably get an award for breathing if it existed! I hate her more than anyone I've ever met.

After class, I headed straight to detention and sat in my usual chair in the corner of the room. I was the only one there. Again.

"Glad to see you made it on time for once," said Mr. Lancaster as he placed a handful of blank sheets in front of me.

Detention with Mr. Lancaster is as boring as watching paint dry. I know, because one time that's exactly what he made me do. He made me sit by a school wall that had been painted and wait for it to dry. But usually he just makes me sit and write lines, like today. I think Mr. Lancaster hopes that if he makes detentions boring enough, I won't want to do another one. But what he doesn't understand is that I don't really mind detentions. My brain calms down and my ears close up and my eyes stop blinking, and instead of seeing the room I'm in or the words I'm writing, I start to see brand-new ways of getting back at everyone. Some of my best, most brilliant ideas have come from sitting in detention.

This detention made me realize that I needed to do something different. Something big. I needed to go outside the box Mrs. Vergara's always talking about—the one inside your head that makes you do the same thing again and again. I needed to try something new. Something that would *really* get everyone talking about me and that would be a hundred times better than putting snakes in the school soup.

I was just thinking about what that big something could be and writing out "I will not put snakes into the school soup" for the fiftieth time, when there was a knock on the door and Mrs. Vergara's head and shoulders appeared.

"Mr. Lancaster, mind if I speak to you outside for a moment?"

"Of course," said Mr. Lancaster, springing out of his chair. Giving me a look that warned me not to try anything, he followed Mrs. Vergara out and shut the door behind him.

Jumping up, I tiptoed over to the door to listen. Mrs. Vergara was probably telling Mr. Lancaster all about the stupid drawing to get me into even more trouble.

Pressing my ear hard against the keyhole, I could just make out their voices. "See here?" Mrs. Vergara was saying. A noise that sounded like large pieces of paper being rustled followed her voice. "He's the only one in the whole year group, possibly even the whole school, to be submitting drawings in this kind of comic-book manga style. For him to create whole characters and a storyline for what was quite a simple project on identity is really quite extraordinary. I think if we entered him he would have a real chance of winning."

"Hmmmm . . ." There were more sounds of paper, before Mr. Lancaster said, "Yes, these are quite something. He's always been rather good at drawing."

I put my eye to the keyhole. But all I could see was Mrs. Vergara's bright blue jeans.

"It's just a shame he's so badly behaved," continued Mr. Lancaster. "The boy's an absolute menace. Snakes in the school soup one minute, beating up the Year Twos the next. In fact, he's probably destroying the classroom as we speak! Imagine if we entered him for a national art award! It would never do. He'd ruin the school's reputation—well, what's left of it."

I pushed my ear even closer to the keyhole. I couldn't believe they were talking about me—and my drawings!

"I was thinking," Mrs. Vergara said, "what if we told him that we *wanted* to enter him, but that we can only do it if he starts behaving? It might settle him. His drawings are already so unique. Really extraordinary. It might give him focus. A reason to engage . . ."

The rustling of papers stopped.

"No," said Mr. Lancaster. "No, Mrs. Vergara. The boy's a lost cause. He would probably sabotage the whole thing and get our school banned from the competition. Bad enough *we* have to put up with him. No reason to force him on to an awards committee and other innocent students."

"I suppose you're right," said Mrs. Vergara. "It's a shame. Such a waste of talent. But—yes, I suppose you're right."

The door handle was suddenly being pushed down. I sprinted back to my corner and jumped into the seat and grabbed my pencil just as Mr. Lancaster came back in. He looked at me and then slowly around the room as if to make sure it wasn't on fire.

"Come on, Hectoooooooor, get on with it. We've both got homes to get to," he said, seeing that I still had at least fifty more lines left to do.

I forced my hand to write as quickly as it could, even though it was shaking and my words were coming out wonky. My face was burning. And with every line I wrote, I thought harder and harder about what I could do next that would be bigger and worse than anything I had done before. Something to show Mr. Lancaster and Mrs. Vergara, and everyone else too, just how much of a menace I could be.

The Trolley Man

"I CAN'T BELIEVE YOU GOT CAUGHT BY MR. LANCASTER AND MRS. BAXTER," said Katie. She was waiting with Will in the playground for me, just like they always did when I had detention. "They're so *old*. You need to be *waaaaay* quicker, H—you're getting slow!"

I looked at the floor. I could feel my face going red. Whenever they think I've messed up, Will and Katie never stop talking about it. Sometimes I'll give them a punch, but I knew this time that Katie was right. I should have been faster.

"Come on! Let's go have some fun with the Year Threes," said Will, trying to cheer me up. "Look, there's Felix. If we're lucky, he might even wet himself a little bit!"

Will gave me a wink. He's always suggesting we do things that will make everyone more scared of us. Will's been my friend since the day we started school together. I saw him flicking bits of eraser at everyone and then lying about it and knew right away that he'd be fun to team up with. Will's like me—well, kind of. He's a bit of a coward and lies a lot, whereas I don't bother lying, not ever. Mainly because it's more fun to see grown-ups' faces when you shock them by telling the truth.

Will's OK, though. He's funny, and he's always helping me spot teacher's pets and brainiacs and show-offs and anyone who has more money than is healthy for them. He's bigger and taller than me, so when we walk around together, every-one knows it's us right away. His hair is bright yellow and straight and sticks up like straw from a scarecrow's head. It makes him look like a bit of a mad scientist. My straight brown hair just flops over my face and halfway over my eyes as if it's too lazy to do anything, so I don't look like a mad anything.

"Go on!" urged Katie, poking me with her elbow and pointing at Felix and his group of tiny friends. "I dare you to."

I glanced around at Mrs. Simpson, who was standing by the gates just ten steps away from us, talking to some parents. It's always tricky beating someone up at dismissal time. If a parent catches you, even Mr. Lancaster gets into trouble, and that means getting detention until he retires.

I looked at Katie. She was challenging me with one of her eyebrows. Katie loves challenging people with her eyebrows. She joined our school last year after she got expelled from another school, and me and Will knew right away that she was one of us. We became friends the moment I saw her using her eyebrows to tell Mei-Li and Robert that she was going to chase them into the next town if they came near her. Katie's super tall and a super-fast runner, so she could probably do it if she wanted to. She has the palest skin I've ever seen on anyone and straight brown hair that looks as if it's been ironed and large square glasses. Normally anyone who wears glasses is a teacher's pet or a brainiac. But Katie is different.

"What are you waiting for?" Katie whispered. "You *are* getting slow!"

That did it. I gave her a scowl and immediately began walking toward my target. But at the exact moment I reached him, Mrs. Simpson turned around. Her eyes fell on me right away, so I had to run past Felix and straight out of the gates to make her think I was late for something.

"Ah man! You waited too long!" growled Will a moment later as he and Katie joined me.

We walked in silence past the candy store on the corner of the street and headed toward the big double road that led to the park gates.

I kicked at some pebbles by my feet. I wanted to kick something bigger and harder.

"What's wrong with him?" whispered Will loudly.

"I don't know," said Katie, only half whispering. "He's

probably just *sore* because he's too *slow* and keeps getting caught."

I darted across the road between beeping cars and entered the park, heading up the gray pathway toward the hill where all the biggest oak trees were. Will and Katie were still talking to each other about me. When they really want to get on my nerves, they pretend to be whispering to each other, without really whispering at all.

"What a sore loser," fake-whispered Will.

"Right," fake-whispered Katie. "You'd think it was *our* fault that he's not fast enough anymore!"

My hands rolled up into fists, and the top of my head felt as hot as a barbeque with fresh-lit coals in it. I wanted to turn around and push Will and Katie as hard as I could so that they wouldn't dare say any of the things they were saying ever again.

We reached the top of the hill, where an old bench stood beneath the oak trees, and that's when I spotted him: the old man. I'd seen him there before, lots of times, sitting on the bench next to a trolley piled high with trash. He was in his usual long, old, crumply black coat that looked as if it had been pulled out from a trash can, and was wearing the bright yellow woolly hat he always had on his head, even in summer. And without even trying, I had the most genius idea that had ever been born. In fact, it was so genius and so out-of-the-box and so unexpected, that I knew it would be enough to make Will and Katie shut up once and for all!

I stopped walking, which made Will and Katie automatically stop too. Will looked at me blankly, but Katie's eyebrows immediately jumped up as if to say, "Yeah? And what?"

"Want to have some fun?" I asked.

Will nodded, a smile breaking across his face and making him look like a hungry fox that had sniffed a chicken coop up ahead.

"See that old man there?" I asked, pointing toward the bench.

"You mean the old trolley man?" asked Katie.

"We're going to let him know he's not allowed here anymore."

"How?" whispered Katie, leaning in toward me. She pushed her glasses up the bridge of her nose.

I waited for a few seconds to keep them guessing and then whispered back, "I'm going to take his *hat*."

"His hat?" asked Will.

"Yup. He's always wearing that gross, stinky hat."

Katie finally smiled, which meant she thought my idea was cool.

"Come on," I said. "Let's go."

When we reached the bench, we could see the old man had fallen asleep. His black-gray fluffy beard was acting like a pillow for his chin as it rested on his chest, and his dirty wool hat was falling to one side like a Santa Claus hat—except it was yellow, not red. He was breathing heavily through his pink-tipped nose, while his half-gloved fingers moved every few seconds—as if they were playing a tune to a song that no one else could hear.

"He's asleep!" whispered Will as we all stood in front of him.

"No way, genius," said Katie, rolling her eyeballs. "What now?" she asked, looking at me. I put my fingers to my lips and then tiptoed my way around the bench and went to stand behind the man. Reaching out, I hovered my hand over his hat, ready to grab it and run.

Will and Katie stared at me. Will's mouth was open, and Katie's eyes were shining like two pools of water that had just been hit by sunlight.

In less time than it took them to blink, I snatched the yellow hat from the old man's head and turned, ready to run. But before I could even take a step, a large hand with dirty fingernails grabbed my shoulder.

"AND WHAT DO YOU THINK YOU'RE DOING?" shouted the old man, leaping to his feet and pulling me back.

Quickly, I threw the hat in Will's direction. It worked. The old man let go of me and ran toward it. But Will was too fast and caught it.

"Want this, trolley man?" teased Will as he held the hat out. The old man reached for it, but at the last second, Will threw the hat to me, laughing.

In a flash, I threw it to Katie, and Katie threw it back to Will. The old man spun around and around, not sure which of us to try and catch first. Then, suddenly, he stopped and looked straight at me. I looked back, straight into his small brown eyes surrounded by wrinkles.

"You," he said, pointing a finger at me. "You give it back!"

I grinned. "Yeah? Make me!" I began spinning the hat around on the tip of my finger like a woolly yellow basketball.

For a few seconds, all he did was stare at me. Then, as swift as lightning, he crouched to the ground and, jumping back up, flicked his wrist toward me with a quick, chopping motion. Something hard stung my face.

Putt-putt-putt-putt-putt!

"Ow!" cried Will.

"Hey! Stop that!" yelled Katie as they both started to back away.

I felt a sting of pain on my leg, and then my face again, and then something hard hit my palm. Closing my hand around a small sharp object, I finally understood what was happening. The old man was throwing tiny stones at us!

"OFF WITH YA!" he cried angrily as his hands magically produced more and more tiny stone bullets. "OR I'LL HAVE YOUR GUTS FOR GARTERS!"

Will and Katie began to run back down the hill under a shower of pebbles, yelping in pain as they went.

I tried to stand my ground, clutching the hat.

"COME ON, THEN," cried the old man. He started to laugh as the little stones flew at me quicker than before. Before I knew it, I had dropped the hat.

He started walking toward me and I quickly realized there was nothing I could do. He was too big to fight on my own—and he was armed too.

"I'LL BE BACK!" I shouted, feeling hot and angry and red as I ran down the hill to where Katie and Will were waiting.

"AND I'LL BE WAITING FOR YOU, YOU LITTLE SCUM!" the old man shouted back as a large stone hit me on the back of my leg.

It wasn't until I reached Katie and Will that I noticed a crowd had gathered. Dog walkers were watching us with their mouths open or frowns on their faces. Their dogs were staring at us too.

"Come on! Let's get out of here," I cried, walking quickly toward the park gates.

Will and Katie followed me out, bowing their heads down low so that no one could see their faces.

But I didn't bow my head low like I should have done. Because I could hear Will snickering and I could see Katie starting to giggle too, and I knew they were laughing at me—again.

"What are *you* laughing at?" I asked, feeling my face burn.

"He got you good," said Will. "Even though he's super OLD!"

"Yeah," said Katie. "And homeless. Talk about embarrassing."

"I'm going to get him back," I said as we hurried out of the park gates. "You'll see."

"Yeah? How?" asked Katie, challenging me with her eyebrows again.

But I didn't know. Not yet.

At the park gates, Katie and Will turned left onto the road that would lead them to their homes. I could hear them still giggling and snickering as they disappeared into the distance. Once they were gone, I looked back over my shoulder and through the railings to the top of the hill. I could see the old man with his yellow hat back on his head, walking away with his trolley as if nothing had happened. As if he hadn't just embarrassed me in front of my friends. I made a silent promise to him right then and there that I would get him back for what he had done, and I would get him back so good that not even stone bullets would be able to stop me.

The Theft of Platform 1

WHEN I GET HOME AFTER A REALLY BAD DAY, ALL I WANT IS TO BE LEFT alone with my computer games. But that afternoon, I couldn't seem to catch a single break. Because as soon as I walked in through the door, before I'd even done a single thing, I started to get shouted at like a criminal.

"HECTOOOOOOR! ARE YOU HOME? *WHY* ARE YOU SO LATE, HUH?"

"I DUNNO!" I shouted back, slamming the front door behind me. I kicked off my shoes and was just about to run up to my room when the voice added, "Your brother made you something, come and see, huh?"

I didn't want to—I wanted to go and start plotting revenge on the old man in the park, but I knew if I didn't go through to the kitchen to see what Lisa was shouting about, she would probably follow me upstairs.

Lisa is my little brother's nanny but is always lecturing me too, so it's like having an annoying teacher in the house. Her real name is Lestari, but we all call her Lisa because that's what Hercules calls her. I try and keep out of her way as much as possible. At home, I try and keep out of *everyone's* way as much as possible. It's just easier.

"What?" I asked, pushing open the kitchen door. Lisa and my sister, Helen, were standing by the kitchen counter in front of a massive plate of grilled cheese sandwiches, and my little brother was sitting on his stool, painting. With glitter. Again.

My brother's name is Hercules. Which makes me just feel sorry for him, because I know he'll get beaten up at school for it. I mean, who wouldn't want to beat up a kid called Hercules? It's a silly name, especially for a four-year-old whose only talent is leaving a trail of glitter wherever he goes. That includes on cereal boxes and the toilet. The problem is, Mum and Dad are fans of old stories about Greek and Roman gods and all the useless things they got up to. So they decided to punish us, their very own kids, with names from their favorite legends.

Hercules and me are named after heroes and my sister, Helen, is named after a Greek woman who had a face that was so beautiful she started a war. The only thing my sister could start with *her* pimply face is a car crash. She's definitely not the most beautiful woman anywhere. Not even in a room she's in by herself. Hercules was a famous warrior, who probably never stuck Legos up his nose or spent his time licking people's hands. And I'm never going to be a hero, even if I am called Hector. So you could say we were all doomed from birth, really.

"Look, Hup-tor! Look!" Hercules cried, holding up a terrible picture. I didn't even know what it was meant to be.

"What is it?" I asked, wondering when he'd start to say my name properly. He made me sound like a burp.

"It's you!" explained Lisa, as if it was a fantastic surprise. "It's great, huh?"

I looked down at Hercules with his brown curls and his chubby cheeks and large brown eyes, and wondered how he could be so happy all the time. It was strange that he never cried—not even when I push him away when he's being annoying and he falls on his bum. Instead of sniveling or telling on me, he always looks at me as if he's trying to remember what happened, and then jumps straight back up.

"Why are your pants so dirty?" asked Helen, looking at me with her eyes narrowed and scratching at an extra-pink pimple. "Did you get into another fight?"

Helen is thirteen. That means she's only three years older than me, but she still tries to boss me around all the time. She acts like she's Mum, so I remind her that she isn't, and that because she isn't, she can't ever make me do anything. Usually all I have to do is call her Pimple Face so that she gets upset enough to leave me alone. Or Dumbo, because of her huge ears. She's a famous teacher's pet at her school, so Mum and Dad are always asking me why I can't be more like her. But I'd rather drink a big jug of slime than ever be like her, and she knows it.

Looking down at my trouser legs, I realized that the stones the old man had thrown at me had left little puffs of white dirt everywhere. I quickly tried to brush away the marks.

"Lisa, look! Look at his trousers. They're all messed up! He was DEFINITELY in a fight!"

"Shut up!" I snapped, brushing harder.

Lisa bent down and grabbed a trouser leg, inspecting it closely like a detective who had lost their glasses. I pulled my leg away from her.

"She's right!" said Lisa, shaking her head and tutting. "Hectorrrr! You were in ANOTHER fight? What will your mum and dad say, huh?"

I scowled, wondering if this day could get any worse. "They won't find out," I muttered.

The best thing about my family is that Mum and Dad are never around. They're always working or going to parties filled with people who think they're clever and are saving the world by eating millions of canapés—that's tiny food that you need at least a hundred of to fill you up. Mum works for a charity that tries to help the environment, so she's always on the news trying to get famous people to do things. One time she met the king of Norway and got some of his army to dress up as giant bees to show everyone how important bees are to the planet, and another time she went on a march with some famous singers to save a forest and they all got arrested. It's super embarrassing, so I pretend she doesn't do any of those things—even though I'm pretty sure everyone at my school knows.

Dad makes documentaries about what he says are "all the souls the world has forgotten." He follows people running away from gangs or being kicked out of their homes by the government and tells their stories, so he's always traveling too. Last week he went to San Francisco for his latest film, and this week he was in Amsterdam, while Mum was somewhere in Scotland trying to turn a castle into a butterfly farm.

Until a few years ago, they used to take us with them when they went to work somewhere nice, but after I nearly set a hotel room on fire one time—by accident!—they never took any of us again. And even when they are home, they're so busy they hardly notice us. Last year they were working in another country on Christmas Day and forgot to call us. Then they felt so guilty that when they got back, they gave me all the games I had asked for, Helen got the new laptop she wanted for school, and Hercules got so much glitter that he could have painted at least three houses with it all.

So instead of Mum and Dad, we have Lisa. And as long as I could make her and Helen forget about the fight, then Mum and Dad would never know.

Just then, the small TV on the kitchen counter started playing a commercial with my sister's favorite pop song in it. Helen ran over to watch, and Hercules began licking Lisa's hand as if it was a brand-new lollipop, which made her immediately start to fuss over him. I grinned, knowing I was safe from Mum and Dad finding anything out about my trousers.

My stomach gave me a kick, as if to remind me I was hungry. I grabbed all the grilled cheese sandwiches Lisa had made and went to the fridge to get a drink. Gaming was always better with grilled cheese and a big glass of something fizzy.

"Hercules! You are our little van Gogh, huh!" said Lisa, giving Hercules a big kiss on the top of his head as he scribbled away furiously making another picture that didn't look like anything that existed in the real world.

"Hope not," I snorted. "Or he'll end up dying penniless too."

"Don't listen to him, Hercules," said Lisa as Hercules frowned. "You finish your drawing while Aunty Lisa gets a packed lunch sorted for your sister's big trip tomorrow, huh?"

"I don't need a packed lunch for tomorrow anymore, Lisa," said Helen, turning back from the TV. "Our book trail's been canceled."

"What's a book tail?" asked Hercules, making glitter circles with his finger over my portrait.

"Not book tail," said Helen. "Book *trail*. It's when you go to places that famous authors wrote about and learn all about them and mark them down on a special map so that you get a prize."

"I want prizes," announced Hercules.

"I want them too," said Helen. "But we can't go now because of the robbery!"

"What robbery?" asked Lisa as I grabbed a can of my favorite drink and pulled open the freezer drawer to see if there was any ice cream.

"Didn't you see the news? Some thieves stole Paddington Bear last night, right from the platform at Paddington Station! And that was supposed to be our first stop tomorrow."

"NO!" gasped Lisa, looking as shocked as if she had made the statue herself.

Helen nodded and spun around on her stool. "Yup! Mr. Wilson said the thieves even took the green plaque that told everyone all about the man that wrote *Paddington Bear*, and the 'Platform 1' sign too, and painted some secret symbols all over the wall in its place."

"Symbols?" asked Lisa.

"Yeah, some secret symbols that apparently homeless people use. None of the cameras caught the thief. Cerys's dad is a police officer, so he knows all about it. And he said that it'll probably get sold underground for *millions* of pounds, because there are only three statues of Paddington in the whole world and that was one of them. And the police think other statues might get stolen too. So the book trail is canceled for now. We can't even go see the Harry Potter trolley at King's Cross."

"That's silly," said Lisa as she tried to stop Hercules from sticking three pens up his nose. "Who would steal half a trolley? No one could ever use it for anything, huh, Hercules?" she added, giving him a wink.

Helen shrugged. She was about to say something else but, on reaching out for a grilled cheese, noticed that they were all gone.

I quickly headed toward the kitchen door with my arms full of everything I wanted.

"Lisa! *He's* taken all the grilled cheese!" whined Helen.

"Hectorrrrrrrr! I made enough for everyone! Give two back, please."

Moving fast, I licked all the grilled cheese.

"Ugh! Why do you have to be so GROSS?" cried Helen as Hercules giggled. I licked them again, which made him giggle even harder.

Helen's face screwed up into a squashed mess of pimples. I grinned and waited. A few more seconds and she would blow—just like a burst pipe.

Lisa sped over to the bread box and cried, "I'm making some new ones right NOW, Helen. Don't worry about *him*!"

Laughing, I kicked open the kitchen door and ran upstairs.

Closing my bedroom door and switching on my computer, I gulped down a whole grilled cheese as the screen came alive. I couldn't wait to begin invading a whole new universe. The *Conquering Hero* series was definitely one of the best games that had ever been invented. Getting to conquer other people's lands and weapons and universes and trying to rule over them and keep control is hard and fun all at the same time. And the battles are the most wicked I've ever played, because there are so many different universes with so many different types of enemies in them.

I'm only four major takeovers away from completing the last level of Universe Four and becoming a champion ruler. No one at school has reached that level yet. Not even in high school.

As I waited for the game to load, I thought about what Helen had said about the thief who had managed to steal a whole statue without being seen by anyone and the joke Lisa had made about the half trolley from King's Cross.

And then, just as my computer screen flashed to life, it came to me! I knew *exactly* how I was going to get my revenge on that old man in the park. The thief had given me a brilliant idea! I would make something disappear without anyone even knowing it was me, just like he had. After all, if I was a menace like Mr. Lancaster said I was, I might as well be the best one there was.

The Runaway Trolley

IT WAS EXTRA HOT AND SUNNY THE NEXT MORNING, WHICH MADE THE concrete playground feel like a bright stone desert and made my legs feel lazy.

Will met me at our usual spot, but he was quieter than normal. I knew he was blaming me for getting us chased out of the park by the old trolley man. Katie was probably thinking the exact same thing, so it was a good thing I had a plan that was going to surprise them! I wanted to tell them both together, but since Katie never came to school on time, I needed to wait until first break.

As we stood against our part of the school wall waiting for the first bell to ring, Will kicked at something invisible on the floor and said, "So . . . did you hear about that robbery last night?"

"Yeah," I said, feeling glad that he had talked first. "But it's just a stupid bear statue from a kid's book. Who cares?"

"Not that one," Will said, shaking his head. "The Paddington statue was the *first* robbery. There was a *second* robbery last night. Some angel statue was taken from that fancy fridge shop in town."

"Fridge shop?" I asked, watching Randy trying to hide behind his dad as he walked through the school gates. Randy was one of our regulars and always paid us with sweets to leave him alone. I gave him a long stare to let him know that I had seen him and that he now owed me three extra bars of chocolate for trying to hide.

"Yeah. You know, Sell-Fridges. They've got a big statue of a queen in front of the shop—except this queen has wings. And she was carrying a tiny angel. That's what the thief stole. Mum can't stop talking about it. She says all the department stores are going to be paranoid now, as loads of them have statues," said Will. I was only half listening now. I was watching Randy trying to disappear into his dad's legs.

"And Mum said the thief left a sign in yellow paint too. Like he's telling everyone he was really there. It's so cool . . . *and* the statue is pure gold. If I was him, I'd break it up into small pieces and sell them off and buy like fifty cars and race them around all day long. Hey, what's that?"

I looked down at my rucksack and saw the corner of Hercules's bandit eye mask poking out.

"Nothing," I said, pushing it and the black hoodie I had stuffed on top of my books back down into my bag. Quickly zipping it back up before Will could ask me anything else, I said, "Look, there's Lavinia. Doesn't she owe us some pocket money?"

Will nodded, following my gaze to the tall, skinny girl who could quite easily disappear behind a lamppost—and often tried to whenever she saw us coming after her. As soon as Will spotted her, we grabbed our bags and chased her until she ended up trying to hide behind a trash can. But before we could get anything from her, the bell began to ring, making everyone stop what they were doing and hurry toward the doors.

"Hey, H," said Will as we waited at the end of all the lines so we could be the very last ones to go in. "We going to get that trolley man back today? How about we collect some leftovers off everyone's plates at lunchtime to throw at him?"

"I've got a better plan," I said, shaking my head. "You'll see."

When we got into the classroom, Will went and sat down at his table on the opposite side of the room from me, and I sat at mine. Mrs. Vergara never lets me and Will and Katie sit together. That's why I have to sit next to Rajesh—who's so scared of me that he just stares at me with huge saucer eyes—and behind Mei-Li, who annoys me with every flick of her ponytail.

"Right, everyone! Homework out, please!" said Mrs. Vergara, clapping her hands. I could see Mei-Li hurrying to rip open her bag and get out her homework book. Mei-Li's homework book was covered with perfect shiny wrapping paper and perfect handwriting and perfect stickers, making it glow like a big square trophy under the classroom lights. It made me want to pull her hair extra hard.

I didn't bother opening up my bag, because there wasn't any point. I didn't have any homework to hand in. Plus, I had a bandit eye mask and a hoodie in there that I didn't want anyone to see.

"Hectooooor?" asked Mrs. Vergara, standing in front of me with an open hand, waiting for me to put something in it.

The whole class turned to look at me, which made me grin.

"Your homework, please. Where is it?" asked Mrs. Vergara.

I shrugged. "Cat ate it," I said. I could hear Will snicker from the other side of the classroom. But he had been a chicken and given something in. I had seen him do it.

"Really?" asked Mrs. Vergara, dropping her hand and her head to one side. "The cat ate your homework *again*? This one really seems to like anything we do on the Tudors, doesn't it?"

"Yes, miss," I said. "I guess it thinks we're doing homework on *tuna*. Not the Tudors."

From somewhere behind me, I could hear Katie start to giggle, which meant she had been able to sneak in without getting caught thanks to me.

Mrs. Vergara's brown skin flushed red. "Up you get," she

said. "You know the drill, so off you go! I haven't got the patience to deal with you today."

I did know the drill, so I got up, grabbed my rucksack, and headed for the door. "The drill" is going and sitting outside Mr. Lancaster's office until he can find time to tell me off and then going back to class so that I can get told off for missing all the lessons I've just been made to miss. I've been doing "the drill" since my first day at school. I actually don't mind it, because I get to skip lessons and watch everyone else going up and down the corridors. And sometimes, if Mr. Lancaster is busy and Mr. Ferguson, his secretary, isn't around, I even get to scare kids passing by as well. I once got three chocolate bars just by sitting outside Mr. Lancaster's office.

But today, instead of watching the corridors to see who I could go after, I decided to use the drill for something else. Sitting outside the main office, I pulled out my half-empty homework book and, turning to the back, began to draw out cartoon strips. It was a plan of what I was going to do to the old trolley man.

After I had drawn three strips that made my plan nice and clear, I waited for the drill to finish. But Mr. Lancaster made me wait so long, I missed first break, and I think he only let me go for lunch because it was probably against the law to starve students—even me.

Catching up with Will and Katie in the cafeteria, I told them all about my plan.

"That's cool!" said Katie. "The old man is going to cry so hard!"

"Yeah!" said Will. "SO hard!"

"You *sure* you can run fast enough, though?" asked Katie. "I mean, *real* fast? Because if you don't and he catches you, you'll be in sooooooo much trouble. Even with the mask on." She leaned forward and stared at me hard through her glasses like two one-eyed goldfishes looking through their bowls.

"I won't get caught," I said angrily. "You'll see!"

I was too annoyed to eat any of the extra pizza slices Katie had stolen off the other tables. I couldn't wait to prove to Katie and Will that I was faster and cleverer than they would ever be! I would show them. I would show everyone! I didn't want to get detention and be kept behind, so all afternoon in class, I sat on my hands and waited for the last bell of the day to ring.

After Mrs. Vergara asked everyone at least 324 questions about things that would never matter, the bell finally rang, and she told us we could all go home. I jumped up first, yelling "Come on!" to Will and Katie as I ran out the door and down the half-empty corridor. All the classes were only just starting to come out. Usually I liked to push and bump people as I walked by, but I was in too much of a rush today.

Katie and Will ran behind me as we made our way out into the playground, through the school gates and across the big road. We slowed down as we reached the tall green gates of the park.

"Keep a lookout," I warned, dumping my rucksack on the ground and taking out my hoodie and Hercules's eye mask. Quickly, I pulled my hoodie on and placed the elasticized band of the bandit mask over my head, lining the eye holes up perfectly. For the final touch, I pulled the hood over my head, just like I had drawn in my cartoon strips.

"Whoa, you look cool!" said Will. "Like Zorro . . . but in a hoodie."

Katie didn't say anything, but I could tell she thought I looked cool too.

I strapped my rucksack back on and grinned at Katie and Will, who both grinned back. I could tell they were feeling as excited as I was now.

"Let's go halfway up and see if he's there," I said as we began walking toward the oak trees and the old man's bench. "Stay in front so no one sees me."

"Where is he?" asked Will, frowning, as we got halfway up the hill.

I looked ahead. The old man's trolley was parked in its usual place right next to the bench. But the old man was no-where to be seen.

I beamed under my mask. This was going to make my plan so much easier! Not only had the old man gone and left his trolley behind, but the park around us was empty of any-one else too. There wasn't even a single annoying dog! It was as if everything was working out for me. Finally.

"Stay here," I ordered, feeling so lucky that I was sure

nothing could touch me. Pulling my hood tighter around my face, I ran at top speed up the hill toward the trolley and grabbed the handles. With a grunt, I pushed it on to the long winding pathway that led down the other side of the hill and deeper into the park. I tried to hurry. But it was much heavier than I thought it was going to be, and the wheels were so old and wobbly that they felt as if they might fall off at any second.

"Hey! What are you doing?"

I looked over my shoulder and saw the old man running toward me from the trees behind the bench. He was carrying a crumpled brown bag in one hand and a half-eaten sandwich in the other, and large white crumbs were falling like fluffy hailstones from his beard.

My stomach jolted as if it had decided to go for a bungee jump without me. I began to run faster, forcing the trolley along the path. Gripping on to the handlebar tight, I tried to steer it toward the trees, but it began to twist and turn as if it had grown a brain of its own.

The old man was still running behind me and shouting louder and louder, but I knew I could outrun him. All I had to do was let go of the trolley and make a dash for the park gates. But no matter how hard I tried to tell myself to do it, I couldn't make my fingers open. The trolley was pulling me along now, instead of me pushing it, and I felt my legs begin to stumble and scrape against the ground. I swung my legs up into the air and tried to balance them on top of the wheels—but they weren't wide enough. And suddenly there was a woman with a dog . . . and a man with a stroller . . . and a kid with a ball!

I began to scream at them to "GET OUT OF THE WAY," but all that came out was: "GETTAAAAAAAAAAAAAAAAAAAA! GETTAAAAAAAAAAAAAAAAAAAAAAAAA! GETTAAAA-AAAAAAAAAAAAAAAAAA!"

"Hey!" cried the woman with the dog.

"WATCH IT!" shouted the man with the stroller.

"Whoa!" said the kid, throwing her ball up in the air and leaping out of the way.

"GETAAAAAAAAAAGH!" I screamed as the trolley roared like a roller coaster down the hill, beyond my control. My hood slipped, and as I tried to pull it back up with my left hand, my right one slid off the trolley handle. Before I knew what had happened, the trolley had escaped and I was flat on the ground.

The trolley shot away like a giant silver bullet and bumped and jumped and rattled and spilled all the way down the rest of the hill. I got to my feet and watched, my mouth wide open, as the trolley's wheels followed the swerve of the path and headed straight toward the lake.

"My trolley! Someone, please!" cried the old man as he cut across the grass and ran past me down the hill to try and catch it.

But the trolley was too quick and everyone was too scared, and as if it had sprouted invisible wings, the trolley flew through the air. A few seconds later . . .

SPLASH.

The trolley had landed smack-bang in the middle of the lake.

I slowly got to my feet, watching as the trolley sank deeper and deeper, and newspapers and plastic bags floated and bobbed like extra-large pieces of brightly colored bread that had been thrown in for a giant invisible duck. Just as it disappeared completely, the old man reached the edge of the lake and stumbled to a stop. His arms were stretched out, as though for a single moment he thought they could still try and catch the trolley somehow. Then they dropped to his side. I waited for him to shout and scream. But he didn't. Instead, he took off his yellow hat and his shoulders began to shake. That was how I knew that he was crying.

"How could you *do* that?" asked a voice from behind me.

I turned round. It was Mei-Li. As I looked back at her, I slowly raised my hands and touched my face where my eye mask should have been. But it was gone. It must have snapped off when I had been thrown from the trolley.

I wanted to tell her to get lost and that it was none of her business and that if she told anyone, she would be in so much trouble she wouldn't know where to run. But before I could say a single word, the woman with the dog who had jumped out of my way, shouted, "Hey! That's the boy who did it!" and began to run at full speed toward me.

I took a look at Mei-Li and then at the woman and her dog, and began to sprint away from all of them, just as fast as I could.

The Two Treasures

"MAN! THAT WAS WICKED!" CRIED WILL.

He and Katie were waiting for me outside the park gates.

I signaled at them to keep on running in case the woman with the dog was still after me, and we sprinted off down the street. We didn't stop until my lungs felt as if they were trying to push themselves out of my chest. I looked over my shoulder while I tried to catch my breath, but there was no one on the road behind us.

"Oh! Oh!" gasped Katie, who was laughing and trying to breathe at the same time. "His—face! And the SPLASH! And the—the way your legs went everywhere!"

"They looked like Road Runner's legs they were moving so fast!" added Will, trying to do an impression of a giant bird with a hurricane for legs.

I smiled back, but I didn't laugh. My plan had gone wrong.

I had never planned on making the trolley sink in the lake. I had just wanted to hide it in the trees and maybe tip some of the stuff out so the old man had to spend ages finding it all again. And I was supposed to disappear before anyone saw my face, like the statue thief. That was the whole point of my hoodie and the bandit mask. Everything—everything!—had gone wrong.

But I didn't want to seem like a loser in front of Will and Katie again. So instead, I pretended that pushing the trolley into the lake had been my master plan all along.

"Yeah. He didn't see *that* coming," I said. "He won't be coming back any time soon!"

"You're a legend, H!" said Will. We had reached his road, so he thumped me on the arm and turned to leave. Giving me a salute, he added, "No one on the planet could top that! We're going to OWN that bench. We should get a sign telling everyone it's ours now!"

"Can't WAIT for the whole school to hear what you did," said Katie as she turned to leave too. "I might even try and get in on time tomorrow, just to spread the word!"

After they left, I decided to take the long way home so that I didn't have to go back near the park. The woman with the dog might have called the police by now. She had gotten a good look at me. And Mei-Li knew it was me too. She would *definitely* tell on me. She hated me almost as much as I hated her. Then the police would find the mask and test it for DNA and come and arrest me at school . . . and I would be on the news and locked up and probably become one of the secret service's top ten criminals of all time. . . .

I hurried home as fast as I could and, when I got in, ran straight upstairs to take off my hoodie.

"HECTOOOOOOOOOOOR? That you?"

It was Dad! But he wasn't supposed to get back from his work trip to Amsterdam until tomorrow.

I quickly kicked my rucksack under my desk and stuffed my hoodie into the back of my wardrobe.

"HECTOOOOOOOOOOOOOOOOOOOOOOOR! COME DOWN, PLEASE! RIGHT NOW!" he shouted. He was calling from his studio. Whenever Dad wanted to see anyone in his studio, it meant trouble. And I could hear the news channels from his multiple televisions playing, even from my room—a sure sign that I was in big trouble. Dad only ever watched the news channels when he was angry.

A horrible feeling began to swirl around in the pit of my stomach. What if there was a live report about what I had just done? A trolley flying into a pond was sure to make the news, especially if someone had recorded it on their phone and sent the video to the reporters.

I slowly made my way downstairs and stood at the very edge of Dad's studio door. The kitchen door was shut, and I could hear Helen and Hercules and Lisa talking about something and laughing behind it. I knew that Mum wasn't home from her trip yet because none of her shoes were lying like abandoned soldiers on the landing. It was just going to be me and Dad.

"Come in," said Dad. He was sitting in his large leather chair.

I took a single step into the room.

"Close the door," ordered Dad. His glasses were perched right on the tip of his nose. Dad always wore his glasses like that, which made them look as if they were balancing on the edge of a cliff, wondering whether or not to jump.

I did as he said and stood looking at my feet. Dad never let me into his studio unless he was angry with me because he said he didn't want me to ruin anything. It was filled with endless piles of books about famous documentary makers, and by the window was a large table that had so many piles of paper on it, you couldn't see the table at all. The walls were all covered with big black-and-white posters of people he had never told me the names of, except for the wall above the desk, which had two large televisions on it. It was the only room in the house that had televisions hanging on the wall as if they were paintings.

"So? Do you have anything to say about what you've done?" asked Dad, watching me from his chair.

I shook my head without looking at him. I wondered how he knew already and how many years I would be grounded for pushing a homeless man's trolley into a lake.

"Mrs. Vergara was rather upset when she rang me. And I don't blame her."

I looked up, my heart screeching to a halt inside me. Mrs. Vergara? How had she found out so quickly? I glanced up at the television screens to see if I really was on the news already. But there was just a woman in a gray suit with pictures of a graph next to her on one screen, and a weatherman on the other.

"She emailed me and your mum the drawing you did," continued Dad, crossing his legs. "She says you haven't even had the decency to apologize."

In a flash, I realized he wasn't talking about the trolley at all! With everything that had happened, I had completely forgotten about the picture Mrs. Vergara had taken from me yesterday. The one that I hadn't even drawn!

"But that wasn't me," I said.

"And I suppose putting rubber snakes in the lunch soup wasn't you either, eh?" asked Dad, calmly raising a single eyebrow.

"Yes, *that* was. But—"

"Not another word, please," warned Dad, making his right hand into a stop sign. "Since you can't say the words, you can write them instead. In a letter."

"Eeeeeeew! I'm not writing a letter to Mrs. Vergara," I cried. "Everyone will think I'm giving her a love letter!"

"I don't care if they think you're proposing marriage. You WILL write it and you WILL give it to her in front of your whole class first thing tomorrow. Unless you want me to ground you for a month *and* confiscate your skateboard and those computer games you love so much?"

I opened my mouth to tell Dad that I wouldn't apologize for anything I hadn't done. Not ever. And that Mrs. Vergara and Mr. Lancaster and everyone else who hated me could all get lost. But before I could say anything, Dad stood up with a sigh and put his hands on both my shoulders.

"Why can't you be more like your sister?" he asked, shaking his head. "Do you know how lucky you are? To have a roof over your head and all the comforts me and your mum can possibly give you? Do you *know* what some people would give just to have a home to get to every night? No, you don't. You should come and meet some of the people I've been filming for my latest project. There are people out there who go hungry for days on end, who have nothing but a street corner for their home, and here *you* are making a complete mess of everything."

I felt my whole face become blood red. I hadn't even known that Dad's new film was about homeless people. I couldn't get away from them. There was a fizzing in my ears, like a firework about to go off.

Dad's gaze moved to something over my shoulder, and suddenly he said, "Here, take a look at this." Turning me around, he pointed to the television on the right and, grabbing the remote control from his desk, increased the volume.

The sound of applause rang around the room. On the

screen, a tall, slim man with wavy gray hair and a big white smile that shone almost as bright as his pinkie ring, was handing a giant check to a short woman in a bright orange cardigan. Behind her, the mayor of London, whose face was always on giant posters everywhere telling us that he was making London better, was politely clapping. At the bottom of the TV screen flashed the words:

SIR NESBIT GIFTS £5 MILLION TO
HOMELESS SHELTER IN ST. ALBAN'S &
BACKS MAYOR BAINBRIDGE'S NEW LAW.

"*That's* the kind of man you should be aspiring to be like," said Dad, his hands on my shoulders getting heavier and heavier. "Someone who *shares* what he has to help make the world better for people. Not worse."

I wanted to say that I didn't see how me sharing my old size 3 sneakers or computer games could ever make anyone's world better, but I bit my tongue instead. I was in enough trouble already—and that was without anyone knowing about the trolley in the lake.

I watched as Sir Nesbit and the mayor proudly pushed the short woman in the orange cardigan to the side and shook each other's hands.

Flicking the screen off, Dad removed his glasses and pinched the top of his nose together with two fingers. That was a sign that my lecture was nearly over.

"You'll write that letter after tea. You'll show it to me. And then tomorrow you're going to give it to Mrs. Vergara and I'm going to check she got it. OK?"

I stood still and didn't reply. I wasn't ever going to write an apology for something I didn't do.

"OK?" asked Dad, louder.

I gave a half nod, with my fingers crossed tightly behind my back.

Just then, Hercules came running into the room and grabbed one of my dad's legs in a hug.

"Daddy! Come and play!" ordered Hercules.

Smiling at him, my dad let himself be pulled out into the corridor without looking back at me. I stayed where I was. I wanted to kick the wall so hard that the whole house would fall down.

Who cared that I hadn't drawn that stupid picture? Or that I hadn't meant to set fire to that hotel room? Or all the other times I had got into trouble without even meaning to? No one. No one cared about the truth; they always instantly thought I was guilty.

So let the woman with the dog and the trolley man and Mei-Li tell on me to the police. Then Dad would see just how much of a mess I could really make! I couldn't wait to see his face. He was out there making stupid documentaries about homeless people, and I was throwing their stuff in the lake.

"Hup-tor! Come on!" said Hercules, jump-hopping back

into the room again and tugging me by the arm. I didn't want to go, but he kept on pulling.

"Lisa's made pancakes to celebrate Daddy getting back early," he said.

Hercules led me to the kitchen, then went and sat on Dad's lap. I didn't want to eat in the kitchen at all, but it was a silent rule in the house that whenever Mum or Dad were home, we all had to eat together.

Lisa put a huge plate of fresh hot pancakes topped with peanut butter and bananas in the middle of the table. The smell of it made my stomach growl.

"Thanks, Lisa. So, Helen, what's all this about your book trip being canceled?" Dad asked as he poured Hercules a big glass of milk.

Helen chewed and swallowed extra fast, as if she couldn't wait an extra second for her mouth to make space for all the important words it was about to say. "It was because Padding-ton Bear got stolen by that thief!" I leaned over and took three large pancakes for myself as she went on in a rush. "So the police are boarding up all the major statues in all the major stations, and the book trail has had to be canceled for every single school in the country. That means we can't get our slip signed to say we've done it and *that* means we can't get any of the Duchess of Wales badges we've been working for."

"What a shame," I muttered, wondering how anyone could care about something so boring. I grabbed another two pancakes, and Hercules copied me and took two too. It made me grin and give him a wink.

"Oh, yes, I heard about the plight of poor old Paddington Bear," chuckled Dad. "And the golden angel from Selfridges," he added, shaking his head. "What strange things to steal."

"The news said that the thief had left special marks that only homeless people understand," said Helen in her extra-annoying know-it-all voice. "In bright yellow paint. Cerys said her dad said that it was definite proof that some homeless bums were doing the stealing."

Hercules giggled and whispered "Bums!" to me. Lisa poured more pancake mix into a hot pan and scolded, "Hercules! Don't say 'bum' at the table!"

"That's right, Hercules, it isn't nice when we're eating," said Dad. "And, Helen, Cerys's dad is wrong to call homeless people that. It's despicable."

"Des-pickle-ball," whispered Hercules to himself as he mashed a banana up with his fork.

Helen nodded. "Sorry, Dad. But do you know anything about those signs? What do they mean? I told Cerys that you would know because of your new film."

Dad smiled and perched his glasses even closer to the tip of his nose. He loved it when Helen was extra sickening and acted interested in his precious films. I never usually listened when he talked about them because they weren't proper real movies like the ones you went to see in the movie theatre.

They just had loads of people no one knew, talking with sad music in the background. But this time I kept my ears open, because I wanted to know about the yellow signs too.

"Homeless people do sometimes draw signs on walls and bridges," said Dad. "It's like a secret code. A way of letting other homeless people know if a place is safe or dangerous. Or if there are people there who will help them or call the police on them. Things like that. It's strange a homeless thief would expose the codes to the public, though. . . . It goes against the rules." He leaned back in his chair. "Did you know, George Orwell was—"

As Dad began to talk about yet another famous person who was so famous I'd never heard of them, I gulped down my last mouthful of pancakes and reached for the milk. The gulp was so loud it made Dad stop talking.

"Hectoooor! Come on, now! Why can't you eat like a normal person?" he asked, shaking his head at me.

"Yeah!" said Helen, neatly putting another slice of pancake into her mouth as if she was practicing to be the next queen of England. "You're like an animal!"

"He's not an ani-mole!" said Hercules, scowling at Helen.

"Hello, my treasures!" sang Mum's voice from down the hallway.

"MUUUUUM!" cried Hercules, jumping down from Dad's lap. Mum threw open the kitchen door and gave him a kiss on the top of his head and then planted another one on Helen's head. "What are you all talking about?" she asked, looking around. Spotting the pancakes, she threw off her coat and grabbed a plate. "Lisa, you star! I've had a beastly day! Is the kettle on by any chance? And, Hectoooor! I got *another* missed call from Mr. Lancaster. Honestly, is it too much to ask that you keep your nose out of trouble for one second?"

"It's OK, Leonora," said Dad. "We've had a chat. Hector's going to be writing a letter of apology to Mrs. Vergara as soon as he's done massacring his pancakes."

Helen gave a snicker. I glared at her and wondered what they would all do if I told them that I had just come home from pushing a homeless man's trolley into the bottom of a lake.

Maybe they wouldn't even be surprised. They already thought I was a menace, just like everyone at school did. And I knew they wished I wasn't around.

So I got up and, leaving them all behind in the kitchen together, ran back upstairs to my room. Slamming my door shut tight, I switched on my computer and pulled my headphones on, letting the sounds of the game drown out my thoughts of everyone downstairs, and the letter I was never going to write, and the homeless thief nobody could stop talking about, and the fact that Mei-Li could be calling the police about me right now. And as I entered my latest universe, I tried my best to forget about the old man in the park too. The one who, thanks to me, would now be sleeping on his bench without a trolley full of rubbish by his side.

The Eyes That Spied

THAT NIGHT, DAD STOOD OVER ME WHILE I WROTE THE LETTER TO Mrs. Vergara. It was only three lines, but they made me want to hurl up my dinner. So before I left for school the next morning, I threw the note away and put the new one I had secretly written in my pocket instead.

I was planning to walk the long way around instead of cutting through the park like usual. But just as I got to the park gates, I changed my mind. I wanted to see if the old man was still there on his bench, or if I had made him leave for good. I didn't want him—or any police that might be there—to see me, so I snuck through the trees instead of taking the pathway.

As I got closer to the bench, I could see that the old man wasn't there. Neither was the dirty red sleeping bag he usually sat in. In his place were two kids from the high school, holding hands and giggling. And there wasn't a police officer in sight.

I had *won.* I had made the old man so scared of me and so sad about losing his trolley full of rubbish that he had left. Will had been right—that bench really was ours now!

I whooped out loud and punched the air, scaring the icky kissers so much that they got up and left. I couldn't wait to tell Will and Katie that I had done it. It didn't even matter that it was a little bit by accident. I was truly unstoppable now.

Making my way out of the park and onto the big road that led to school, I headed to the sweet shop that stood on the corner. It's the only sweet shop near to school, so it's always super busy. It's called McEwans Delights, even though Mr. and Mrs. McEwan are two of the scariest and strictest sweet shop owners in all of history. They only ever let four children into the shop at a time, and Mr. McEwan watches at the door to stop anyone from sneaking in and making it five. Mrs. McEwan treats everyone as if they're a potential armed robber—even grown-ups—and watches them so closely that sometimes the smaller kids run out without even buying anything.

I hardly ever have to go in, because of all the sweets and chocolates I get from everyone else to make me leave them alone. Last year, I got so many sweets that I had to store them in a huge box under my bed. No one knows it's there except for Beatrice, the cleaning lady, and Hercules. I think Lisa knows about it too but she's never said anything, and Hercules is good at keeping secrets, so I let him take what he wants so long as it's not my favorite chocolates.

Today I felt like celebrating my victory over the old man, so I decided to stop by the sweet shop and see who was outside. Maybe I could make someone give me their fizzy cola bottles. As I got closer to the shop, I could see Mr. McEwan in the doorway surrounded by a puddle of bobbing heads, shouting, "Oi, there's four already in here! Don't even try it, missy, or you'll be banned."

I looked around for someone with a bag of fizzy cola bottles. They came in a golden-brown plastic bag that I could spot a mile away—and usually sniff out too. And then I spotted him: right in the middle of the group of kids Mr. McEwan had been telling off outside the shop. The curly brown head of Jason Slater! He was two years below me and one of the smallest boys in school, so he was easy to pick on—and I knew he liked fizzy cola bottles. Shoving everyone else to the side, I headed toward him.

But just as I was about to put my hand on his shoulders, I saw something bright and luminous yellow flash behind him.

It was a police officer, and she was kneeling and talking to someone.

And that someone was sitting on a dirty red sleeping bag.

At that moment, Jason Slater must have felt me standing behind him because he suddenly turned around and, with a small shriek, chucked his bag of candy at me and ran away. His best friend, Diana, looked down at her bag of candy and chucked it at me too before running off to catch up with him.

But I didn't care about the sweets anymore. I kept staring at the police officer's bright yellow back and her round black hat as she nodded and said words that I couldn't hear.

I craned my head to see better without getting too close.

It *was* him. The old trolley man. And suddenly he was looking straight at me with his deep brown eyes. Then the police officer had turned around and was looking at me with her bright blue-gray eyes too!

I took three small steps back, and when the police officer didn't tell me to stop, I took off, running up the road toward school, checking over my shoulder every few seconds to see if she was behind me. But she wasn't.

"Hey, what's up with you?" asked Will as I crashed into him outside the front gates.

I was too out of breath to speak. I wanted to tell him that the old man wasn't in the park anymore but was at the sweet shop instead. Except all that came out was "He's—he's moved. . . ."

"Huh?" said Will, his face scrunched up like a finished bag of chips.

Before I could get my breath back, the school bell began to ring. I glanced behind me again, but no officer in a bright yellow jacket was in sight. Maybe I was safe. Maybe the old man had got confused with so many kids from my school everywhere. He was old after all. He probably hadn't even recognized me outside the shop.

It wasn't until first break that I was finally able to tell Will and Katie everything that had happened. Usually we would be chasing down Randy and getting everything he owed us, but this was more important.

"And now he's outside the McEwans' shop!" I finished. "He must be sleeping there now."

"So he's actually living *closer* to school?" asked Katie.

I nodded. "Think so."

She shrugged. "Still, what's he going to do? You were wearing your mask and hoodie the whole time. He didn't see your face. No one did. And even if they had cameras in the park, the police wouldn't ever be able to recognize it was you."

Cameras. I hadn't even thought of that! Katie didn't know that my mask and hood had fallen off, and she didn't know that Mei-Li had seen me, or the woman with the dog. I didn't want to tell her either.

"Yeah. That police officer was probably just telling the old man to get lost and move on," said Will. "They do that all the time. It's their job. So nothing to worry about."

But I couldn't help worrying. I needed to cover my tracks—which meant I had to find Mei-Li right away and make sure she had kept her mouth shut. I looked around the playground for her. I couldn't see her anywhere, but I could guess where she was.

"I'll see you in a bit," I told Will and Katie. "I've got to go and, er . . . get something."

"Hey, what about Randy?" asked Katie. "We're behind schedule!"

"You go get him," I shouted over my shoulder as I headed into school. Running down the corridor and up the stairs to our classroom, I stopped outside the door and peeked in through the glass window.

Mei-Li was there, just like I thought she would be, with her best friend, Rania, and brainiac Robert and Mrs. Vergara. They were arranging a display of books on a shelf, alongside a sign that said "BOOKS TO INSPIRE YOU THIS MONTH," and were chatting and laughing as if it was the most fun way anyone could ever spend a break time. It made me wonder how they could be so clever and so dumb all at the same time.

"HECTOOOOOOR! What are you doing here? Spying on your class, are you?"

I jumped and looked around. It was Mr. Lancaster.

"No, sir. I just forgot something."

"And what would that be, then?" asked Mr. Lancaster, standing so close to me that I could see his nose hairs moving.

"My . . . chips . . . ," I said, just at that moment remembering the letter in my pocket too. "For break time. I need to have some every break, or I could faint."

"Faint? From a lack of chips?" asked Mr. Lancaster, frowning.

I nodded. "Yup. They're baked. Not fried, see, sir? So it's like having one of my five-a-day veggies."

"Hello," said Mrs. Vergara, swinging open the door and smiling at us both. "I thought I heard talking. Do I have another helper?"

I shook my head as fast as I could without it falling off.

"He came in to get his chips," said Mr. Lancaster. "Apparently he could faint if he doesn't have them."

"Ah," Mrs. Vergara said with a sigh. "I thought it might have been for something else." She looked at me with her eyebrows raised. "Something you might have *forgotten* to give me this morning?"

I made a silent groan. My dad had obviously told her to expect a letter from me! Wishing Mr. Lancaster wasn't standing next to me, I got the crumpled letter out from my pocket and handed it over.

"There it is," said Mrs. Vergara, her eyebrows climbing back down their invisible ladders. "How lovely!" Then opening it up, she began to read it right away.

I watched nervously as Mr. Lancaster leaned in and read it too. But for teachers who expected us to read whole books in just a few days, they seemed to be taking forever. I leaned in too to see what was taking them so long. All I had written was:

> *Dear Mrs. Vergara,*
>   *Everyone is always saying we should never lie,*
> *but if I said I was sorry for doing that drawing I*

didn't do (the one with smoke and fire coming out
of your bum), then that would be a lie.

So this is a not-sorry letter because I didn't
draw that drawing that you want me to be sorry
for, and if you want to find out who did it, I think
you need to launch a full Investigashon and maybe
call in the FBI too.

From Hector

P.S. If I had drawn the drawing, I would have
made your bum much smaller and the flames
coming out of it much more real.

"I see . . . ," said Mrs. Vergara, frowning as she folded the letter back up. Her lips and her face were twitching so much I didn't know if she was happy with the letter or if I was about to get another detention because of it. I looked at Mr. Lancaster. His mustache and nose hairs were twitching too. "Right, well. Thank you for this," Mrs. Vergara said. "I'm glad you told me how you feel, and I'll, er . . . see what we can do to investigate the matter further. Now, you better go on in and get your chips. We wouldn't want you fainting, would we?"

Holding the door open, she watched as I went inside and slowly walked over to my rucksack. Immediately, like mice who had noticed a cat, Mei-Li, Robert, and Rania stopped what they were doing and watched me too.

"Actually, Mrs. Vergara, I was just on my way to speak to you—in private, if I may?" said Mr. Lancaster. Mrs. Vergara nodded, followed Mr. Lancaster outside, and pulled the door shut behind her.

I knew I had only a few seconds, so I took my chance. I walked up to Mei-Li and, ignoring Robert and Rania, said, "You'd better not tell anyone what you saw yesterday."

To my surprise, she stared back at me, not looking even a little bit scared. I took a step closer to her, but she glanced toward the classroom door and, raising an eyebrow, took a deep breath as if she was about to shout for Mrs. Vergara.

I knew a threat when I saw one. I scowled and took a step back.

"I'll find you later," I hissed. "And if you tell, you'll be in trouble."

I turned to leave, when she said loudly, "No. YOU'RE the one who's going to be in trouble."

I spun back around to stare at Mei-Li. Robert and Rania were both staring at her too, with their mouths wide open.

"What did you say?" I asked, feeling my face and ears start to heat up.

"I said, YOU'RE the one who's going to be in trouble!" said Mei-Li, taking a step forward. "Not me. What you did to Thomas was horrible!"

"Who's Thomas?" I asked, surprised.

"The man whose trolley you pushed into the lake," said Mei-Li.

"You be quiet," I warned Mei-Li. "Or else."

"No," said Mei-Li. "I *won't* be quiet. I'll tell EVERYONE! *We'll* tell everyone," she added, pointing to Robert and Rania, who instantly turned as white as paper. "Unless . . ."

She paused.

"Unless," she said slowly, "you apologize to Thomas and replace his trolley!"

"What?" I asked, wondering if Mei-Li had gone completely nuts and forgotten who she was talking to. I could tell Robert and Rania were wondering the same thing.

I was about to tell her that there was no way I was going to do *either* of those things when Mrs. Vergara opened the door and told me to get back outside if I wasn't planning on helping.

I walked toward the door, and when I reached it, I turned to give Mei-Li a warning look. I told her with my eyes that she had better do as I said or else. But she was looking straight back at me, as if she wasn't even a bit afraid, and giving me a look that said exactly the same thing.

Eros's Missing Bow

"YOU COMING OVER TO MY PLACE TOMORROW?" ASKED WILL AFTER school was finally over and we were all on our way home.

I was glad it was Friday. The week had been way too long, and I was tired from keeping an eye on Mei-Li and Rania and Robert the whole day.

As we passed the corner shop, I slowed down. I couldn't see the old man. Thomas, Mei-Li had said his name was. I wondered how she knew what he was called.

"He's not there," said Katie, nudging me with her elbow. "See! You *have* scared him away."

"Yeah," added Will. "He knows not to mess with you!"

Grinning, I kicked a stone across the pavement in front of me.

"So you both coming tomorrow, then?" asked Will again.

"Nah, can't," said Katie. "Dad's got me this weekend."

Will shrugged and then looked at me.

"Yeah." I nodded. "Mum and Dad are going to be away. I'll bring my board."

"Cool," said Will as we headed into the park. The old man's bench was empty and he was still nowhere to be seen, so I jumped up on it and did a little jig, beating my chest and making loud howling sounds like a wolf to make Katie and Will laugh. I would have done it for longer, but I saw the woman with the dog who had chased me out of the park yesterday, and she was looking at me with a frown. Jumping back down, I told Will and Katie that I needed to be home and, hoping the woman hadn't recognized me without my hoodie and my bandit's mask, ran out of the park.

The next day, after Mum and Dad had pretended they were sad to be leaving us for another work trip, I grabbed my skateboard and headed to Will's house to play computer games. When Mum and Dad are home, they always want me to stay in on the weekends and do homework. But Lisa's too busy with Hercules to notice if I'm in or not, so when it's just her, I get to do what I want. I think she secretly likes me being out of the way.

I like going to Will's place. His mum makes us loads of snacks and talks about murder mysteries as if they're real, and Will's dad is really cool. He gets a new car every year and is always taking Will out to see soccer matches and tennis matches and horse racing. Last year, he took Will to see a real live car race at a huge stadium outside of town. Will wouldn't shut up about it for weeks. It would have been cool to talk with his dad about those kinds of things, but he's always too busy when I'm over.

After we had played computer games for a few hours and Will had lost to me in nearly every game, we had some snacks and then headed outside to go skateboarding around the local streets. Will lives just a few streets away from a community center. There's always loads of kids to pick on outside it. Especially in the afternoon at around one o'clock, when the streets get flooded with kids in bright tights leaving ballet or drama classes. But today, there was no one.

"Center must be closed," said Will, looking at the empty streets. "Shall we go to the park?"

I shook my head. "Nah, it's boring and there'll be fifty million dogs around today."

"Oh, yeah," said Will, leaning against a wall. He didn't like dogs, not since he had been chased by two massive poodles whose tennis balls he had nicked. I didn't want to go to the park because the woman with the dog might be there, or the old man.

"Shall we go to the high street?" asked Will.

I shrugged. "That's boring too." As I rolled my skateboard

back and forward with one foot, I watched a bus slowly pass by. "Hey, I know! Let's get the bus and go boarding on that bit next to Big Ben."

Will hesitated. Last summer his mum had found out we'd been taking the bus into the city on our own nearly every day and had screamed so much that we might as well have been trying to board a plane to China.

"Come on," I said. "It's only a few stops."

"All right," he said at last. "But we can't stay too long. I need to get back for the match. It's West Ham against Newcastle United! The biggest match ever in premiership history. Dad's bought us special T-shirts to wear."

"Yeah, it's gonna be a good one," I said, pretending that I would be watching it too. "Don't stress. It's not even two o'clock yet, so we've got loads of time. Come on!"

Will gave in, and minutes later we were jumping on to the 159 bus that had grumbled to a stop in front of us.

"Age?" asked the driver, looking at Will with a frown, as you have to be ten years old or younger to ride for free.

"Ten," me and Will said together. Will was always getting stopped on the buses and at cinemas for looking older. The driver stared at us and our skateboards for a moment and then waved us through. We went and sat on the upper level, laughing at the people we could see on the streets below as we passed endless rows of shops and bridges and the roof-tops of cars, until the robot bus voice called out: "Next stop,

Westminster Station." Me and Will pressed the buzzer as many times as we could before the stop arrived to annoy the driver, making her shout at us from behind her glass cage as we leapfrogged out the back door. There's nothing funnier than getting shouted at by someone who can't run after you.

Crossing the big city road that surrounded Big Ben like a moat, we popped down our boards and immediately began to whizz and rattle and roll our way over the miles of nearly empty pavement that lay right next to the River Thames.

Me and Katie and Will had found this place completely by accident last year, when we had spent the summer trying out all the different buses. Out of all the bus routes we tried, the 159 was the best one, because in just half an hour we could leave our boring part of town and be right in the middle of London, next to the river and Big Ben and the best place for skateboarding. We spent whole days skating past boats and statues and bridges and cyclists who dressed funny. And when we got bored, we skated up to all the big lights in Piccadilly Circus and got ice creams and watched the weird people who painted themselves in gold and silver to pretend they were statues standing outside the theaters. Sometimes we had to run away from police officers wandering around because they hated skateboarders, but that only made it more exciting.

After we had done eight races right up to Piccadilly Circus, we stopped to get ice creams and ate them sitting on the top step at the base of the famous fountain. It shouldn't have been famous because there was never any water in it, but everyone came to see the statue on top of it. All around us, huge groups of tourists were stopping to look up and take pictures of the glistening winged man. He was wearing half a robe and standing on one leg on top of a swirl of black waves that rose straight up like solid water being shot two stories high. Every now and then, a gross couple would kiss each other and cry out, "He's got me! I'm in love!" as they filmed themselves being pretend-shot by the statue, who was holding out a bow. It really did look as if he was getting ready to aim an invisible arrow down into the crowds below. As we were finishing our ice creams, a couple next to us began to kiss so loudly that they sounded like broken hoovers and I heard Big Ben begin to strike in the distance.

Dong . . . Dong . . . Dong . . . Dong . . . Dong . . .

"Oh, man, it's five already? I'm going to be late!" said Will, jumping up. "The match starts in less than an hour. Come on, let's go."

"I'm going to stay," I said. "I'll go home in a bit."

Will frowned. "You're going to stay here all on your own?"

"Yeah," I said. "I want to practice my flips some more."

"OK . . . ," said Will, not sounding too sure. He walked off to the bus stop, looking back over his shoulder at me. I knew he thought I was going to get into some major trouble, but the truth was, there was no one who would notice whether I was back or not.

I don't know how long I spent rolling up and down and

around the embankment trying to learn new tricks, but I had just done a double flip trip and landed on my deck perfectly, when I realized that the buildings and the pavement had all gone from being sunny and loud to being dipped in shadows and nearly silent. The streetlamps and the balls of light by the river had switched on too, and the roads were nearly empty. I had never stayed out so long in the city all on my own before, but I wasn't scared. Not even a bit. I was hungry, though, so I began to roll my way back up to Piccadilly Circus. I thought I could get a snack and see the big screens lit up in the dark while I waited to catch the bus home.

As I made my way past all the restaurants and pubs that lined the streets, I could hear the sounds of people shouting and cheering and booing from inside. The soccer match must have gone into extra time, because it felt as if everyone in London was still watching it except me. I had never seen the city so empty. But it was brilliant, because it meant I could make giant zigzags on the road with my board and not crash into anyone.

I bought a bar of chocolate from a corner shop and found the bus stop I needed. Sitting on the bench, I waited for the 159 heading toward home to arrive. The bus stop lights weren't working, but the giant screens were so bright and quick, I felt like I was sitting in the middle of a silent laser show.

It was strange sitting on my own, especially with the roads being nearly empty too. All the big shops had shut, and the crowds of tourists, whose feet usually beat the pavements like a thousand small drums, had disappeared.

After watching the adverts on the big screens so many times that I knew them by heart, I began to wonder if the buses were even running and, if they weren't, how I was supposed to get home. I couldn't skateboard all the way home—not when I didn't even know the way. I was about to go back to the corner shop and ask the woman if she knew if the buses were running, when I saw something that made me stop.

In the doorway of a big old building directly opposite me, I could see a dark shape lying on the ground. As I watched, it began to move. Gradually, like a weird human plant, the shape grew into a figure of a tall, skinny man dressed in a long, rumpled black coat and a dirty woolly hat, whose whole face was covered in a big bushy beard.

I sat extra still and held my breath and squinted my eyes to try and see his face properly, but with the darkening of the dusk sky, all I could make out was the shape of the hat—and the beard too . . . a hat and a beard that I knew right away.

It was Thomas.

I kept completely still. Telling my muscles not to move and my heart to stop beating in my throat, I watched him shake his arms and legs as if they were stiff, and slowly emerge from the doorway.

I wondered what was he doing here. Had he followed me and Will so that he could get his revenge on me? Was this where he was living now? Had he seen me? Was he going to come over? And if he did, what was I going to do?

I wanted to get up and jump on my skateboard and get away as fast as I could, but I couldn't move. My brain was telling me to do things the rest of me couldn't. All I could do was sit and wait to see what he would do next.

The old man lifted his hands in the air and did a long stretch. He looked up and down the street as a motorcycle roared by. Then, before I even knew what was happening, he broke into a run.

I shrank back against the bus shelter, my heart thumping so loudly I was sure it was using speakers. By the time I realized he wasn't running toward me at all, he had sprinted right past me, to where the giant billboards were, and had stopped to stare at them. I leaned forward and looked up too, but they were only showing the same swirly adverts for burgers and flowery perfumes they had been showing all day long. Along with the big calculator-y numbers that told us it was now 8:41 PM.

I carried on watching. I could only see the side of his face, but I could tell he was smiling. Maybe it was from the way his beard moved. After a moment, he turned from the screens and glanced around, as if wanting to make sure he was alone. As he looked in my direction, I quickly dipped back behind the plastic wall of the bus stop and waited for a few seconds before peeking out again. He had gone back to looking at the billboards. A taxi swished by. And now there was no one else around. There was only the two of us.

As I looked on, the old man stretched out his arm. He had something in his hand, something that glinted and shimmered in the light of the flashing billboards. I was too far away to see what it was, but I heard it make a loud *click.*

In the very next instant, the gigantic screens and the streetlamps and the lights shining out of the building windows around us—all of them switched off at exactly the same time, plunging everything into a bucket of pitch-black darkness.

I rubbed my eyes and looked around, but I couldn't see a thing. It was as if the whole city had been turned off and smothered with a giant black pillow. The darkness was a darkness I had never seen or felt before—not even in a power cut when somehow, your eyes can still make out shapes. There wasn't a single light around. Not a single car or bus or tinkling cyclist or voice. Nothing. Just darkness.

I blinked hard to try and make my eyes see again. After a few seconds, first the road and then the shops and the railings and the pavement all began to form shapes in front of me, but only in confusing shades of hazy gray.

From somewhere nearby, I could hear the sound of something whirring and buzzing. I strained my eyes in the direction of the noise and saw a shower of orange-yellow sparks, raining down like a magical waterfall. It was as though someone was setting off tiny fireworks that weren't quite reaching the sky.

Tiptoeing out of the shadows to get a better look, I could see the dim shape of the fountain—the one that me and Will had been racing around all afternoon. The sparks were coming out right from the top of it and . . . and . . . I rubbed my eyes, hard, to make sure they weren't playing tricks on me. But they weren't. *He* was there! The old man was hanging from the neck of the statue like a spider, throwing out sparks of fire that left trails of light like a fading web.

The whirring and the sparks only lasted for a few more seconds before there was a loud metal clank: something had fallen from the top of the fountain into its wide round basin. The sprays of orange-yellow light and the buzzing noise stopped and the old man jumped down, using the statue's shimmering black ledges and carved out waves as footholds. It didn't take him more than three short jumps. Rattling a tin can loudly in his hand, he sprayed something on the steps of the fountain. He stood back, waited for a moment, and then lifted his hand again. Another *click*, and instantly, all the streetlamps and screens and building lights flashed back on, hurting my eyes with the punch of their brightness. The large electric clock on the bottom of the billboard blinked back to life.

I stared. If its time was still right it was now 8:42 p.m. Only a single minute had gone by.

I willed myself to creep back into the shadows, but I couldn't move. So I stood as still as I could, holding my breath. The old man didn't look my way—not even for a second. Instead, he gave a deep, loud chuckle that echoed around the empty streets and, taking off his hat, gave a long, slow bow to the billboards and another to the fountain. Then, scooping something up from the basin of the fountain, he stuffed it under his coat and ran off down the street, melting into the darkness.

I slapped my cheeks just like my dad did when he was putting on aftershave and felt the stings on my skin. I definitely *hadn't* been dreaming. Everything I had seen had actually and really happened!

For a few seconds, everything stayed still and quiet. Then, from behind me, I began to hear the sounds of the city again. First came the footsteps of someone walking toward the bus stop; then a woman talking on her phone; and the echoing tunes of a stereo blasting loudly from a brightly colored rickshaw being cycled up the road. But they had arrived too late. No one else had seen what I had!

Slowly, I left the bus stop and crossed the road to the fountain. All afternoon, I had seen tourists taking selfies in front of it because they thought the statue on top was Eros— a Greek god who liked flying around and shooting arrows into people to make them fall in love. But I knew it wasn't really him, because of Mum and Dad's obsession with ancient

Greece. They'd told us a thousand times that the statue was actually of Eros's brother, Anteros, who also liked shooting arrows at people, but as revenge for them not loving someone back. But none of that mattered now. Because whoever was standing up there, his bow was missing. And on the steps of the fountain where I had been sitting with Will just a few hours earlier, were three diagonal lines, sprayed in bright yellow paint.

Hidden Figures

"HECTOOOOOOOOOOOOOOR! GET UP! YOU'RE LATE FOR BREAKFAST!"

With a groan, I shouted back that I didn't want any breakfast and pulled the covers tighter over my head.

It had taken me ages to get home the night before, and when I finally did, Lisa and Helen spent what felt like an hour telling me off for being so late.

I raised my right hand in front of my eyes. It was still there: a streak of yellow paint on my palm from where I had touched the steps of the fountain. The mark told me it had all really happened and that my brain wasn't playing tricks on me.

"HECTOOOOOOOOOOOOOOOR! DON'T MAKE ME COME UPSTAIRS!"

"Fine! Coming!" I shouted, even though I wasn't. Instead, I kicked away the covers, got up, and went and switched my computer on. After it had beeped to life, I typed in my password. But it didn't work.

I tried it again . . . but it still wouldn't let me in.

"LISA! WHY'S MY COMPUTER NOT WORKING?" I yelled.

And then I remembered. Last night, after Lisa had finished yelling at me, she had rung Mum and Dad so that they could yell at me too. They'd been so angry that they had told Lisa to change my password so that I couldn't play any games, and said that they were going to cut their trip short to come home and have a "serious word with me."

I kicked my side table, making my lamp fall over. It was so unfair!

"OI, LOSER," shouted Helen as she thundered past my door on the way to her room. "LISA'S CALLING YOU. AND MUM AND DAD ARE BACK ALREADY!"

Ignoring her as she slammed her door shut and turned her radio on, I headed downstairs. I knew Mum and Dad were going to be mad at me for making them have to come home early, so I hoped they would already be too busy working to notice me getting my breakfast. Dad's studio door was half open, and I could hear him speaking loudly to someone. But I didn't know if it was Mum, so I crept up to the door and peeked around the edge.

Dad was spinning around in his chair on the phone, and Mum was on the window seat, drinking tea and reading the paper.

"Christian, I say let's go with Mary," Dad was saying. "Her story's more interesting. Plus, we can use her as a bridge to highlight the robbery in Piccadilly Circus last night. Doesn't she sleep near there?"

I paused outside the door.

"Don't forget the signs!" Mum whispered.

"Oh, yeah! And then we can get Mary's viewpoint on the symbols left at the crime scene—and how she feels about the newspapers attributing these thefts to the homeless. . . ." Dad paused to listen. "Exactly. It's not like any of these items will be easy to sell on. All very mysterious. Especially since not a single soul seems to have seen the thief."

Except for me, I thought.

I listened for a few more seconds, but Dad started to talk about backers and funders, so I headed for the kitchen.

On the kitchen table I could see the rest of the Sunday papers. The statue theft had made every single front page, and one had even put out an appeal for more information. I wondered what they would give me if I told them what I'd seen. Maybe they would make me famous and give me an award. That would show stupid Mr. Lancaster and Mrs. Vergara that I didn't need *them* to get awards! And I bet they wouldn't give me as many detentions if I was famous either.

I looked down at my hand. The mark on my palm was evidence I had been there, but I needed more. I had to try and find the old man so I could tell all the journalists at the papers where he was. And that meant leaving the house, which wasn't going to be easy after getting grounded only last night. I would need to be extra nice to Mum and Dad and even Lisa to get them on my side.

In the kitchen, Lisa was on her own, peeling carrots by the sink. Walking up to her, I gave her a big smile and said, "Good morning, Lisa."

"Are you sick?" she asked, putting down the peeler and frowning at me. I shook my head.

"Well, hurry up and eat breakfast. I need to use the table for lunch prep."

"Hup-tor!" cried Hercules, running into the kitchen with a huge toy airplane in his hand. Jumping up and down next to me as I poured out my cereal, he tugged at my arm. "Can I have some?"

I shrugged and gave him my bowl, which made him immediately drop his plane and shove a handful happily into his mouth.

"HECTOOOOOOOOOOOOOOOOOOOOR! NO! HE CANNOT HAVE THOSE!" shouted Lisa, taking the bowl from Hercules. "Too much sugar!"

As Hercules began to cry, I gave Lisa a scowl. Grabbing my bowl back, I headed out of the kitchen.

"HECTOOOOOOOOOOR," shouted Lisa again, following me into the corridor and looking up at me through the banisters.

"WHAT?" I asked, trying to resist the urge to pour my cereal over her head.

"Your dad has promised Mrs. Sanders that you will be helping her out today—as part of your punishment for yesterday. You're to go over there this morning, OK?"

Mum and Dad were always making me and Helen help Mrs. Sanders. She lived down the road and smelled of unwashed socks and vinegar. Helen actually liked helping her because that's how sad she was, but I only went when Mum and Dad forced me to as a punishment.

Usually I hated going, but today it was just what I needed! Mrs. Sanders was so old she would never know how long I had stayed with her. Just as long as I did whatever she needed me to quickly, I would have time to go look for the old man. I would go and check the bench in the park first, and if he wasn't there, then I'd check by the sweet shop too.

"Ugh, fine," I said, trying to sound miserable. "I'll go right now."

As I ran up to my room, I could hear Lisa half muttering, "Well, wonders will never cease!" as she headed back to her carrots and Hercules.

Once I finished breakfast, I pulled on my black hoodie and jeans and grabbed my skateboard. Mum and Dad always made us have Sunday lunch at exactly one o'clock when they were home, so I had to be back by then, which meant I didn't have too long; it was already nearly ten, and I had to make time for Mrs. Sanders's chores too.

I pulled open my rucksack and chucked out all my

schoolbooks, then packed it with some sweets and chips from the box under my bed in case I got hungry.

"Where are YOU off to?" asked Helen as she caught me heading out the front door. "You're grounded, remember?"

"I've got to go help Mrs. Sanders, stupid!" I said, trying my best not to grin.

Skating away from Helen's speechless face, I headed straight up the road, and before reaching Mrs. Sanders's, took a sharp detour into the park and up the hill to the old man's bench. But there was no one there.

I looked around to see if there was anyone in a long black coat and a woolly hat nearby. But there were only joggers in bright-colored clothes that stuck to them like wet tissue, and people throwing balls and sticks for their dogs, and the ice cream truck coming to a stop in its usual place between the lake and the wooded area of huge oak trees.

Jumping back on my skateboard, I skated as fast as I could to McEwan's Delights. The old man wasn't outside. Mr. McEwan wasn't outside either, because there weren't any other kids around for him to yell at. But maybe the McEwans knew the old man—they were way too strict to let anyone sit on the street outside their shop without permission. Unless *they* were the ones who had called the police officer in an attempt to get rid of him too! Still, it was worth a shot, so pushing open the shop door, I walked inside.

"Yes?" asked Mrs. McEwan sharply, her eyes prodding me with invisible questions. "And what do *you* want?"

"WHO IS IT?" shouted Mr. McEwan from somewhere in the back.

"IT'S THE SNATCHER KID," shouted back Mrs. McEwan, still staring at me. "YOU KNOW? THE ONE THAT ALWAYS SNATCHES THINGS OFF THE OTHER KIDS."

"Oh?" Mr. McEwan came out to the counter. He looked hard at me. "What do you want?"

"That's just what I asked him," said Mrs. McEwan.

"Well," said Mr. McEwan, rolling his eyes, "now *I'm* asking him!"

They both turned to look at me, waiting.

"Please, er . . . sir . . . and, er . . . Mrs. McEwan. . . ." It felt weird trying to make my voice nice, rather than shout back at them like I usually did. "Do you know the man in the yellow hat? The one who was sitting outside the shop on Friday?"

"You mean Thomas?" asked Mrs. McEwan, her frown deepening. "The man whose trolley you pushed into the lake?"

My mouth fell open.

"That was a nasty thing for you to do," said Mr. McEwan. "Pushing someone's property into a lake like that. Especially a man who's lost so much already."

I opened my mouth wider to tell them it was the old man's fault for throwing stones at me and my friends. But then I remembered what Mei-Li had said and it gave me an idea.

"I know—but I didn't mean it," I replied, wondering if they would believe me. "And I want to tell him how sorry I am, and that I'm going to try and get him a new trolley."

"Oh, well! Isn't that one for the books?" asked Mrs. McEwan, poking Mr. McEwan on the arm.

"All right, all right!" said Mr. McEwan, rolling his eyes again. "I heard it too!"

Leaning over the counter, Mrs. McEwan looked at me over her glasses. I could see the tiny hairs on her upper lip and what I'm pretty sure was some tuna stuck in her teeth.

"Sometimes he sleeps down the high street," she whispered. "Outside the police station if he can get a spot."

"Why are you whispering?" asked Mr. McEwan.

Mrs. McEwan shrugged. "It's more exciting."

"Er . . . thanks," I said, heading toward the door.

"What do you know," I heard Mr. McEwan say. "The snatcher kid actually said 'thanks'!"

"Only took him four years, bless him," replied Mrs. McEwan as the door shut behind me.

Hopping on my skateboard again, I zoomed and zigzagged down the pavements that led to the high street, thinking about how strangely happy Mr. and Mrs. McEwan had sounded when I had said thanks. It seemed to make them like me. Even though they knew it was me who had pushed the old man's trolley into the lake.

Coming up to the police station, I rolled to a stop. The station stood right on the corner of where the high street started and was one of the biggest buildings in our whole area, almost as big as school. It was made of bright red bricks and shaped like half a circle, with lots of doors and archways. I must have walked past it at least half a million times since I had been born, but I had never seen people sleeping near it.

When I reached the steps leading up to the main doors, I looked up. Through the big, shiny glass doors, I could see police officers standing at the counter. But there was no one outside.

I walked over to the next big doorway. There was no one there either. Just a big blue door that was chained shut. And there was no one at the doorway next to that one either. After that, the rest of the building was gated off, so I walked back around to the front, passing the main entrance again to check the doorways on the other side. In one of them, there was someone lying on a large piece of cardboard, asleep.

I climbed up the steps to the arch and tried to see if the person was wearing a yellow hat, but whoever was sleeping there had covered themselves right up with a large gray blanket.

Not knowing what else to do, I coughed loudly.

The person under the gray blanket didn't move.

"Hey," I said. "Hey. Are you Thomas?"

There was still no movement, so I nudged them with my foot. "Hey. Wake up!"

Suddenly a large hand shot out and grabbed my ankle.

"What'd you think you're doing?" said a rumbling voice. The blanket slipped down and I saw a man's face, but this face didn't have a dark bushy beard or a hat on its head. It had a short, rough brown beard and sharp gray eyes, and it was wearing a baseball cap that said "Forever Young."

"Hey," I said, trying to snatch back my sneaker with my foot still inside it. "I was looking for T-Thomas."

"Yeah? Well, you best do it without kicking the likes of me, eh?" said the man as he angrily pushed my foot away, almost making me stumble backward down the steps. "What'd you want with Thomas anyway?"

"Nothing," I said. "I just need to . . . find him."

The man narrowed his eyes so much that I wasn't sure they were even open anymore. "You're the kid who pushed his trolley into the lake, aren't you?" he said, sitting up to look at me properly.

I stared back at him. How did *everyone* know about me and the trolley?

"Yeah," I said. "But I didn't mean to," I added, not lying.

"I'm guessing you don't know what you made him lose that day," said the man, shaking his head at me.

I wanted to ask him what was so special about a trolley full of newspapers and some plastic bags, but instead I said, "I wanted to tell him that I was . . . you know, sorry."

The man said, "Hmmmmm," and looked at me again from my head to my shoes. I could feel his eyes scanning me like a machine, trying to decide if I was telling the truth. I made my face look sad and serious.

"Well, he won't be on the buses, not on a sunny day like

86

today. I'd head to the train station. Down the alleyway where the pizza shop is. Sometimes he hangs out in the back there. And listen . . ."

He leaned forward and I took a step backward.

"You better never touch any of us with your foot again, yeah? We might be sleeping rough, but we're not here to be treated rough. If you try it again, you might not get your foot back. Got that?"

I looked down at my right foot and quickly nodded.

"Off with ya, then."

"Th-thanks," I said.

"That's 'Thanks, *Sam*,'" said the man, narrowing his eyes again. "My *name's* Sam."

"Thanks, *Sam*," I said, before running back down the steps and quickly hopping on to my skateboard again.

I zoomed down the high street and up the hill to the main train station. Sam had said there was a little alleyway between it and the pizza shop, but I had never seen one before. It was there, though; I had just never noticed it.

Popping my skateboard up into my hands, I examined the alleyway. It was so narrow it looked like someone had forgotten to brick up a large gap in the wall between the two buildings. It was dark and filled with dirty grass and weeds, but it had to lead somewhere because I could see light at the end of it.

I hesitated. I needed to go and help Mrs. Sanders out, or

else I'd get into even more trouble. But I just needed to see if he was there. It would only take a few seconds. And if he was there, then I'd go straight to the police station and tell them everything I had seen last night and where to find him and tell them to tell the papers too. Taking a deep breath and holding all the air in a ball in my mouth, I ran down the alley as fast as I could, until I got to the end where a large courtyard was waiting.

Directly behind the back wall of the train station, hidden in the corner of the square, was a tent with the front zipper wide open. In front of it were two old foldout chairs, and in one of them was an old woman with black coils of hair that sprung out in all directions and bright purple gloves that had no fingers to them. She was surrounded by at least thirteen cats who were all meowing and stretching and yawning and prowling about.

Catching me staring at her and the large fat ginger cat she was stroking, she looked back at me with a frown.

"What are YOU looking at?" she asked, her face squashing itself into a thousand wrinkles. "Go on! Off with you. I'm not here to be stared at!"

"I wasn't staring," I said, trying to look somewhere else and wondering why she was so angry at me when she didn't even know me.

"Oh, yeah! Just coming to kick one of my babies for a bet? Or spit on me? Don't think I don't know your lot. Always harassing me after school. Now you've got to harass me at the weekends too, eh?"

"No—no—I just—"

"Well, I won't take it no more! I've had enough of you lot!"

I didn't know how to prove that I wasn't one of the kids she was talking about. Then I remembered that whenever Dad saw a homeless person on the street, he always offered them a sandwich or a coffee, which made them thank him loads.

"I—look, I have these. . . ." Quickly unzipping my rucksack, I took out a bag of chips and held them out to her.

"Salt-and-vinegar chips?" she asked mockingly.

"I've got cheese-and-onion too," I tried.

The woman stood up and the cat sprang forward. "Go on!" she cried. "Off with ya! Kicking my cats and making my life hell first and wanting to give me charity second! Don't think I don't see through your games!"

The cats were hissing at me almost as angrily as she was. She was obviously too mad to help me. And I was running out of time to go to Mrs. Sanders's house and still get home for lunch. Grabbing my skateboard, I backed away from the woman and hurried down the dark passage, emerging seconds later into bright sunlight on the right side of the alleyway.

5

Into the Woods

"RIGHT IN THE MIDDLE OF LONDON, AND NO ONE SAW *ANYTHING*," SAID Katie.

She had said the same thing about forty times that day. And she wasn't the only one who was talking about it. All anyone at school could talk about were the three strange robberies and the "invisible" thief and the bright yellow symbols that had been left at the crime scenes. Mr. Lancaster had even made a sad joke about it in assembly, warning us not to start stealing each other's exam papers because they were the most valuable things any of us had. Nobody had laughed. Not even Mrs. Dawson, who laughs at everything. Even fire alarms.

"We were right there! It would have been so cool if we'd seen something," said Will, kicking a stone and hitting a girl on the shin with it. I could tell it was by accident, but when the girl looked at us, Will gave her a menacing look, as if it had been on purpose.

"Apparently he knows how to get all the police cameras to stop working. Imagine seeing how he does that . . . ," said Katie in a dreamy voice.

As Katie and Will started talking about all the things they would do if they had the power to switch off the world's CCTV cameras, I looked around the playground for Mei-Li. I bet that she could help me find the old man. I just had to make sure no one saw me talking to her. There would be nothing worse than being seen talking to a teacher's pet.

I finally saw her in the corner of the playground, where the teacher's pets were playing one of their boring lunchtime games. This one involved trying to kick a tennis ball and running around seven bases. Except none of them could kick or catch to save their own lives, so they spent forever at each base or standing around giggling.

Mei-Li was standing next to the starting base, whispering to Robert and Rania. Just as I spotted her, she looked over at me.

I wanted to look away, but for some reason I couldn't. So I scowled at her. Then, without any warning, she started walking toward me. So did Robert and Rania, although they looked far more frightened than she did. I had given Robert at least thirty super wedgies, so I knew what he looked like when he was scared.

They came to a stop in front of me. Will and Katie stared down at Mei-Li as if she were a bug that had appeared out of thin air.

"What do *you* want?" I asked. My cheeks felt as though someone had placed two freshly microwaved plates right on top of them.

"I need to talk to you," said Mei-Li.

"What do *you* need to talk to *us* about?" asked Katie.

Mei-Li shook her head. "Not you," she said to Katie. "Or you," she added, looking at Will. "Just you," she said, pointing at me.

Will snorted as if he couldn't believe what he was hearing.

Robert whispered, "Danger," through the side of his lips and took a scared step backward. Over Mei-Li's shoulders, I could see other kids in the playground starting to look our way. I had to end this, quickly.

"Fine," I said. "You've got twenty seconds." I gave Will and Katie a nod to let them know to leave us alone.

"You heard him," said Will, pushing Robert farther back as Katie did the same to Rania. Once they were far away enough not to hear me, I whispered, "What do you want?"

"I heard you went all over town looking for Thomas yesterday," said Mei-Li.

"What? How'd you know that?" I asked.

Mei-Li didn't answer me. Instead she asked, "So you *really* want to say sorry to him, then?"

I nodded, making a sad and serious face like I had done for the McEwans.

Mei-Li looked at me so hard that she pretty much used up all her twenty seconds. Finally, she seemed to come to a decision.

"OK. Meet me by the park bench after school. I'll help you find him."

"Really?" I asked. I couldn't believe Mei-Li was so stupid that she had actually believed me and my face.

"Yeah," she said. "So long as you do *everything* I say. After all, you wouldn't want me and my dad telling *your* dad what you've done. Would you?"

"What's that supposed to mean?" I asked, feeling confused. "What does your dad have to do with anything?"

"You'll find out IF you don't apologize and make it up to Thomas properly," said Mei-Li, grinning. "Catch you after school, then! ALONE."

I opened my mouth, but nothing except a puff of hot air came out. My brain had gone blank. Turning on her heels and giving a flick of her ponytail, Mei-Li walked back to Rania and Robert, who both looked like they had been turned half to stone by their own personal Medusas. Everyone else in the playground began to go back to their games, but they were still watching me out of the corners of their eyes.

"What was all that about?" asked Katie, with a frown so deep it looked as if it might never leave her forehead.

"Nothing," I said, telling my brain to think fast and come up with something to say.

Katie and Will looked at me in confusion, before Katie gave a loud gasp.

"Hold on! She's not trying to be your . . . *girlfriend*, is she? Eeeeeeeew!" cried Katie.

"NO!" I said. "That's *disgusting*!"

"Yeah! Yeah, she is!" said Will, jumping up and down and pointing at me.

I shook my head and punched Will on the arm as hard as I could. "Shut up!"

"Hey," said Will, rubbing his arm.

"All right, calm down," said Katie, surprised at how angry I was.

Will and Katie didn't ask me anything else after that, but for the rest of the day, I could tell they were watching me and Mei-Li closely, like two really rubbish spies.

At home time, after we had chased some Year Three kids all the way to the sweet shop, I told Will and Katie I had to get home quickly and left them. Sprinting to the old man's bench, I saw Mei-Li was already there. She was sitting and reading a book. Like the nerd she is.

"Finally," she said when she saw me.

"What? I'm not even late!"

"All right. No need to get all *crocodile-y* and snap at me," she replied, standing up.

Feeling an urge to push her to the ground, I stuffed my hands in my pockets. I wanted to frighten her in some way—and show her that she couldn't talk to me like I was stupid. But she knew too much.

"How did you know I was looking for the old—I mean for Thomas?" I asked. It had been bothering me all afternoon.

Mei-Li tilted her head to one side and looked at me just like Mrs. Vergara did—as if she was trying to multiply a really long number in her head. "Me and my dad volunteer in the soup kitchen off the high street—it's where all the local homeless people go. Dad's friends with everyone and everyone tells him *everything*."

So homeless people *did* have a secret network! Only they were called soup kitchens. I wondered if the police knew about that already.

"But how does your dad know my dad? My dad doesn't work in a soup kitchen." Not that I knew of anyway.

"Because of his new film," said Mei-Li. "He's spoken to us on the phone, and he's going to come and film us soon."

I made a "pah!" noise, which came out louder than I thought it would. And before I could stop myself, I said, "Why'd he want to film *you*? You're just a boring teacher's pet."

My words made Mei-Li's cheeks flood with color, like two cups being filled with bright pink lemonade. "Because he *likes* me, and he told me that I was important and should be in his film," she snapped.

I scowled at her. I felt another urge to kick her in the shins. She had spoken to my dad—and he had actually *liked* her and asked her to be in his stupid film. He had never asked me anything like that! Not ever. I guess I wasn't important enough for him.

"Whatever," I said. "Just show me where Thomas is."

"Fine," she said. "Let's go." But instead of turning to leave the park like I had thought she would, she began to make her way down toward the lake.

"Where are you going?" I asked, trailing after her. I wondered if this was a trick and Mei-Li and her dad and their secret homeless society were planning to push me in the lake for revenge.

"To Thomas," she replied, followed by something that sounded like "Duh!"

"But he doesn't live in the park anymore. I checked yesterday."

"Thomas doesn't just stay in *one* part of the park, you know," explained Mei-Li. "He likes to sleep in the bit under those trees too. Except when it gets too cold and starts raining. Then he sleeps on the night buses."

"How do you know all that?" I asked.

"He's my friend. I've known him for almost a year now. Ever since Dad started working at the soup kitchen."

Walking right around the lake, we reached the tallest group of oak trees in the park, all standing at attention like an army dressed in a uniform of green leaves. Mei-Li headed straight into them, and as the trees got so big and tall that even the sunlight had to fight to make its way through, I saw it: a small green tent and, beside it, a tall figure sitting on top of a red sleeping bag, wearing a crumpled black coat, tatty white sneakers, and a woolly yellow hat.

"Hi, Thomas!" said Mei-Li, waving as she jumped over a log to join him.

The old man stood up with a smile. "Well, hello, my little lady! What brings you here?"

Mei-Li waited for me to reach them before answering. "Thomas, this is Hector, from my class at school. He wanted to meet you. And, Hector, this is Thomas. The man who you need to apologize to."

A Tale of Three Lives

"APOLOGIES?" ASKED THE OLD MAN, SOUNDING CONFUSED. HE WAS holding out a hand for me to shake. But he smelled bad and I was sure his hands were super dirty, so I gave him a wave instead.

"No worries," he said. "Don't have to shake if you don't want to . . ."

Then, slowly, the old man's eyes began to get wider and wider.

"Hold on!" he said. "*You're* the boy. The one who pushed my trolley into the lake!"

"He's come to say sorry," explained Mei-Li, reaching out to touch the sleeve of the old man's coat.

"Yeah, I'm sorry," I said, trying to look how I imagined being sorry looked. "And it was an accident!" I added truthfully.

"An accident?" shouted the old man, his whole face

becoming blotchy and as purple as beetroot. "You mean to tell me I *didn't* see you go up to my bench, grab the handles of my trolley, and run off down the hill with it until it crashed into the lake?"

"No! I mean, yes, I pushed the trolley away from the bench," I said. "I just wanted to hide it in the trees. But . . . then I kind of lost control of it."

"So apparently, he didn't *mean* to push it in the lake," clarified Mei-Li, like a judge in a courtroom.

Thomas shook his head and stroked his beard angrily. "Well, I don't believe him. I've seen him around, and I've seen what he does to the other kids. He's a bully. A *lost cause*! And worse than that, he's a bully who thinks it'll make him look good to go messing with a homeless guy's most precious possessions." He took a step closer. "Isn't that right, boy? Aren't you just a plain old *bully*?"

I glared back at the old man. My legs began to tremble, and my ears felt like they were going to pop right off like two rocket launchers. "Yeah! Well, at least I'm not a THIEF!" I screamed.

"What did you say, boy?" asked the old man as Mei-Li stared at me in confusion.

"You heard me!" I shouted. "I SAW you! On Saturday night, next to that fountain in Piccadilly Circus—and now that I've found you, I'm going to go to the police and tell them it was you. YOU'RE the thief everyone's looking for!"

The old man gazed down at me with a blank face and then, turning to Mei-Li, asked, "Is he off his rocker?"

"I'm not off anything! I saw you—in the exact same coat and with your beard and everything!" I shouted. "You even had your hat on!"

"My hat?" asked the old man, pulling the hat off his head and looking down at it.

I frowned, because something was different. His hair looked much darker than it had been on Saturday night . . . but then I realized it must have looked lighter then because of all the light from the screens. "Yeah! You were wearing that exact same hat. Probably another thing you *stole*," I added. "Along with all those priceless statues."

The old man looked at Mei-Li again, and then at me, and then at his tent, and finally started to laugh.

"Ah Lord . . . that's a good one! Me! The statue thief! He actually thinks I'm the statue thief!" Falling quiet, he suddenly grabbed me by the arms. "Boy . . . ," he whispered, bringing his face so close to mine that I had to turn away from the smell. "You think if I had stolen a load of plonking big statues, I'd be living like this?" He turned around so that I could see his sleeping bag and his tent, which I now noticed had holes all over it. "This is my home. And *this* is where I was on Saturday night! Not near any blasted fountains."

I wanted to move away, but his grip on my arms was too strong.

"Here," he said, standing back up straight and taking

something small, square, and brown out of his pocket. He tossed it to me, but I missed, and it fell to the ground in front of my feet. "Go on. Take a look and see the two reasons I'd *never* steal anything!"

Mei-Li watched me with narrowed eyes as I picked up the object from the floor. It was a wallet, just like the one my dad had. Except instead of being filled with money and credit cards, it was stuffed with pieces of paper and newspaper cuttings.

As I held it up, the wallet fell open. On one side was a clear plastic window that showed a faded piece of pink card, half burnt on the bottom. On the bit that wasn't burnt was a photo of Thomas that must have been taken about a hundred years ago—when he had lots of curly hair on his head and his face had been shaven clean. Above the photo were the words:

UK DRIVING LICENCE
1. Chilvers
2. Thomas Benjamin, Dr.
3. 01/01/1976 UNITED KINGDOM

Opposite it, underneath another cracked bit of clear plastic, was an old photo that looked as if it had been folded and unfolded at least a thousand times. It showed a woman with short red hair, kissing a baby's bald head. The baby was laughing at the camera with both its hands in its mouth.

"Who are they?" I asked, pointing to the woman and the baby.

"My two reasons. I would rather live on the streets and have them be proud of me than ever live the life of a thief," said Thomas. Snatching his wallet out of my hand, he gently put it back in the pocket inside his coat.

"Mei-Li, get him out of here," he said, turning from me and waving us away. "And don't ever bring him back. I don't want little *snots* like him making fun of me and throwing my things around and then coming here and insulting me to my face."

"Sorry, Thomas," Mei-Li said softly. "I thought he really wanted to apologize." Grabbing me by the sleeve, she ordered, "Come on." But before pulling me away, she stopped and took something wrapped in tinfoil out of her rucksack. "Dad sent you your favorite," she said to Thomas, putting it on top of the sleeping bag. "Chocolate spread and banana."

The old man gave her a nod, still not looking at me.

As we hurried back out of the trees and toward the lake, Mei-Li said, "So I guess you never wanted to say sorry to him at all, did you?"

"Yes I did!" I said, stopping in the middle of the path in front of her.

"No," said Mei-Li, shaking her head. "You just wanted to accuse him of being the statue thief."

"Well, I DID see him there," I argued. "And I think we should tell the pol—"

But Mei-Li didn't let me get any further. "Don't even think about it. I know Thomas, and I know he would never *ever* steal anything, so you just leave him alone. And leave me and everyone else alone too!"

Pushing me away with both of her hands, she stormed off up the hill.

"But wait! Who was that woman and the baby in the photo? And why was he so mad about losing his stupid trolley?"

Mei-Li ground to a halt. Slowly, she turned round, breathing so hard through her nostrils that I wouldn't have been surprised if flames had come out of them, and marched right up to me.

"That photo is of Thomas's wife and his baby daughter," she said, shouting at me as though I wasn't standing right in front of her. "They died in a car crash years and years ago. Thomas was driving the car."

"Is that why he became . . . you know?" I asked.

"You mean *homeless*?" asked Mei-Li, not yelling now but somehow sounding even angrier. "It's not a dirty word, you know!"

I wanted to tell her that the word might not be dirty, but Thomas definitely was, but I knew she wouldn't answer any more of my questions if I did.

"So . . . why did he become *homeless*, then?" I asked.

"Because sometimes people can't take the sadness. Not when someone they love dies. They get *too* sad." Calming down, Mei-Li sighed. "At least that's what my dad says. And that's what happened to Thomas. He felt sad and alone, and there was no one to help him. He got so sad that he lost his job, and then he lost his house, and then he was sleeping in a car but he lost that too. So he had to start sleeping on the streets."

"Oh," I said, feeling my nose begin to run for no reason. I wiped it with the back of my sleeve.

"That's why he lives in this park and loves that bench," carried on Mei-Li. "It was where his wife liked to sit. Satisfied?"

I shrugged.

"And as for your last question. That trolley was full of newspapers. Thomas collects them from all the trash cans in the park. He takes them to the recycling center and they give him some money. That's how he makes enough to buy food every day. But it also had something else. . . ."

"What?" I asked. "The plastic bags?"

Mei-Li shook her head. "No. Not just the plastic bags! There was a photo album right at the bottom of the trolley. It was full of pictures of his wife and daughter. And now he won't ever get them back because of *you*."

I looked over Mei-Li's shoulder to the lake and felt my nose run so heavily that I needed both my sleeves to dry it. There was a long silence.

"Don't go near him again," said Mei-Li finally, looking down at the ground instead of me. "He doesn't deserve anyone who's not going to be nice to him. I should never have taken you to see him. Because you're not just a bully. You're a *liar* too."

And with that, Mei-Li walked away, her head high, leaving me standing alone, staring at Thomas's old bench.

The Thin Blue Line

THE NEXT MORNING, I AVOIDED THE PARK ON MY WAY TO SCHOOL. I
didn't want to think any more about Mei-Li or Thomas or the
questions that had kept popping into my head all night.

I arrived early and waited for Will at our usual wall, scowling at anyone who dared to look at me until he joined me.

"Hey! Did you hear what happened last night?" asked
Katie, suddenly appearing from the crowds and running up
to us. Me and Will looked at each other in surprise.

"How come you're so early?" Will asked.

Katie shrugged. "My brother gave me a lift."

We didn't say anything. Katie hated anyone making a fuss.
Even when her half brother, who lived in another country,
had come home and given her a lift to school for the first
time in years.

"Anyway, did you hear?" asked Katie again. "The thief
stole Tinker Bell! I just heard it on the news in the car."

"Tinker Bell?" asked Will, looking at Katie as if she had gone nuts.

"Yeah, you know, from *Peter Pan,*" said Katie. "There was a tiny golden statue of her outside that famous children's hospital—Great Osmond's Street or something. And the yellow marks were left everywhere again."

"If I was the thief, I would have just taken the vending machines," said Will.

"Why?" asked Katie.

Will shrugged. "Sweets and chips and stuff are loads better than some weird fairy statue."

"Did they get any pictures of the thief on CCTV or anything?" I asked.

Katie shook her head. "No, nothing—again. But the head of the police was on the radio and he said they were going to start rounding up homeless people for questioning. That means they suspect them—because of the yellow signs. And then Mayor Bainbridge came on and said he was going to help to get all the criminals off the streets by making a new law. Hey, Will, how would you steal a vending machine anyway?" She narrowed her eyes. "And who's that new boy?"

I wanted to ask Katie what else she'd heard on the radio, but I could tell she wasn't really listening anymore. She was too busy staring at a boy with a shiny new rucksack and imagining how much pocket money he was going to give us.

I followed Katie and Will as they both ran after him. But

all through class and even at lunch, as I smashed trays into people's chests and took sweets and money from kids as usual, I was feeling strange. No matter how much I didn't want to think about them, Thomas and the pictures in his wallet kept popping back up in my mind like a jack-in-the-box.

By last break, I was feeling so strange that I let Randy go before he had even had a chance to pay us.

That was when I realized something was seriously wrong with me.

"Are you ill?" asked Will as we watched Randy running away from us with a look of happy shock on his face.

"Yeah, I think so," I said. My insides felt like fruit getting mashed up in a blender.

"Ew, well, don't give it to us," said Katie, covering her mouth and taking a step back from me.

"Don't worry, I won't," I said, suddenly wishing I could make her and Will disappear.

"It's that Mei-Li, isn't it?" asked Katie. "*She's* making you ill. She keeps staring at you weirdly in class."

I was about to tell her that she was wrong, when the bell began to ring. But as we walked back to class and sat down at our tables, I spotted Mei-Li staring at me with a funny look on her face, just like Katie had said. She quickly looked away when she saw I'd noticed. I waited for her to look back at me again so I could silently tell her to leave me alone, when Mrs. Vergara shouted, "Right, class, listen up! Instead of our reading time today, we've got some special guests coming in to talk about a rather big issue facing our city at the moment. And that's the issue of . . . crime."

Instantly a whole classroom of eyeballs swiveled over to me and Will and Katie. I narrowed my eyes and gave everyone a death stare.

"As you will all have heard, London is currently unfortunately being vandalized by a thief, or a gang of thieves, who are going around stealing very precious objects—objects that belong to the public," said Mrs. Vergara.

"The Invisible Thief," cried out Nelson from behind me.

"Well, yes, that's one name for him—or her." Mrs. Vergara smiled. "Among others. But we all know that no one can ever really be invisible, don't we?"

Nelson nodded but looked disappointed at the news.

"Now, the mayor of London and the police are trying their best to catch this thief and would like to teach us how to become more vigilant." She went to the classroom door and opened it, and two police officers walked in.

Everyone immediately sat up straight and tried to look as if they had never done a single bad thing in the whole of their lives.

"Officers, all yours," said Mrs. Vergara, nodding at them as they went and stood by the whiteboard.

After Officers Philip and Miriam had wasted everyone's time trying to be cool and funny, they finally started to talk about the one thing we all wanted to know about: the Invisible Thief.

Except they didn't really tell us anything. All they said were things like "Any kind of crime needs to be tackled by all of us as a community," and "Theft of any property will not be tolerated by the police," and "Your city is our city, so it's up to all of us to protect it."

After a while, I stopped listening until I heard Officer Miriam say, "So there you have it!" She was pointing to what she had written on the whiteboard. "If you see anything strange, just remember 'POP TARTS.' **P**erson, **O**bject, **P**lace, **T**ime, **A**larm, **R**eport, **T**ruth, and **S**afety! OK. Now, who would like to ask us a question?"

Nearly everyone's hands shot up into the air like arrows being fired straight into the sky.

"How come you haven't caught the thief yet? Can he really make himself invisible?"

"Why are all the signs in yellow?"

"Are you going to arrest everyone who's homeless?"

"If the thief's homeless, where's he putting all the stolen stuff?"

"How much is Paddington Bear worth?"

After telling us that no one could become invisible and that homeless people weren't going to be arrested just for being homeless, and that they had no idea how much Paddington Bear was worth, Officer Philip turned to Rajesh, who was making squeaking noises and reaching up so high he looked like he was trying to dislocate his own arm.

"Yes, son, what's your question?"

Rajesh dropped his arm on the table with a thump, and asked, "Are *Big Issue* sellers needed for questioning too? Because there's three of them next to my mum's office!"

I found Rajesh saying "*Big Issue*" in his snotty voice funny, so I muttered out loud, "More like Big *Tissue* sellers!" which made Katie and Will and someone else behind me start to giggle.

Officer Miriam frowned at me, and I looked down quickly at my hands and pretended not to see her.

"You think this is funny, son?" asked Officer Philip. I could tell he was staring at me too, even though I couldn't see him. Instantly the whole class fell quiet to see what I would do next.

"Not your son," I said to the table.

From somewhere in front of me, I heard Mrs. Vergara sigh loudly.

"What's your name?" Officer Philip took a few steps forward and stopped in front of my desk. Rajesh gave another squeak and tried to move as far away from me as possible.

I looked up at Officer Philip's big light-bulb-shaped nose, and replied, "Hector."

"Hector what?" asked Officer Philip.

"No, Hector Landis," I replied, making myself want to laugh.

"Got ourselves a clever clogs here," said Officer Philip, shaking his head. "Someone who thinks it's smart to cross the thin blue line."

"Yeah, well, I'm smarter than *you*," I replied, before I could help myself. Everyone gasped, and someone at the back of the class whispered, "Oooooooh."

Folding his arms, Officer Philip tilted his head to the side. "How do you figure that, then, young man?" he asked.

I glanced around the room. Not a single person seemed to be breathing, and even Mrs. Vergara's bangs looked like they were leaning forward to see what I was going to say next. I could see Mei-Li narrowing her eyes at me as if she was trying to warn me to keep quiet. But I knew I was right. I had the answer, and she didn't and neither did the police. She had been too stupid to see Thomas for what he really was. Well, she was going to know the truth now. Everyone was! I wasn't going to just cross the thin blue line—whatever that was. I was going to jump right over it and pay Thomas and Mei-Li back.

"I'm smarter than you because *I* know who the Invisible Thief is," I said, folding my arms right back at him. "I've seen him *and* I know how he turns all the lights and cameras off too. I saw him do it."

"No way!"

"He can't have!"

"It's a lie!"

"He never!"

"What an idiot."

Officer Miriam stepped forward through all the whispers. "*Did* you see something, Hector?" she asked.

"Hectorrrrr," warned Mrs. Vergara. "This is no time to lie."

"I'm NOT a liar," I cried out, sitting up straighter in my chair. "I was there, on Saturday, at Piccadilly Circus skateboarding and I saw him, but he didn't see me. Ask Will," I added, pointing to Will. "We took the bus into the city and then I stayed behind on my own and that was when I saw the thief take the bow thing from the statue on the fountain!"

Everyone turned to look at Will, who instantly turned a bright shade of green grape.

"I— Yeah— We went there . . . ," he stuttered, nodding.

The two officers frowned at him and then looked at each other. When they had finished, they turned to Mrs. Vergara.

"Mrs. Vergara, if you don't mind, we'll take this young man out into the hall to ask him a few questions."

"Of course," Mrs. Vergara said. "Hectaaaaahhhhhhh," she added, making my name into one long sigh. "Off you go."

I stood up slowly and screeched my chair extra hard as I tucked it under the desk. I could tell the whole class thought I was messing around, but I wasn't. As I followed the officers out of the room, I grinned extra wide, especially at Mei-Li's shocked face, ready to prove just how much smarter than everyone else I really was.

Hercules and the Toy-Lets

BY THE TIME THE FINAL BELL FOR DISMISSAL RANG, EVERY TEACHER AND every kid in every year knew I had been taken out of class by the police.

I could have easily told them all exactly what I had said to the police, but I knew it would be a lot more fun to keep it a secret. Secrets give you power—just as long as you don't give them away too soon. Mrs. Vergara and Mr. Lancaster and some of the older kids were already looking at me different, and I wanted to keep it that way for as long as I could.

"So come on! What did you see?" asked Will, catching up with me as I rushed out of the playground. Behind us, kids from the lower years who were usually too frightened to come close to me, were hurrying after us, trying to eavesdrop.

"And why didn't you tell us?" added Katie, clutching her rucksack straps as she jogged up to us.

"I'll tell you everything tomorrow," I promised as I broke out into a run. I needed to get to the park as soon as I could to see if the police had listened to me and had gone to arrest Thomas.

"Wait," shouted Katie. "Why can't you tell us now?"

"GOT TO GET HOME," I yelled back. "I'LL TELL YOU TOMORROW!"

Ignoring the stares from everyone standing outside the McEwans' shop and the deep frown that Mr. McEwan was giving me, I sprinted at top speed across the big road and into the park.

I looked around, expecting to see bright yellow police tape and vans with flashing lights and officers crawling across the park like a billion black ants.

But things in the park were as boring and as normal as always. People were walking children home from school and pushing strollers and playing with their dogs and jogging like puffing machines. There wasn't a single police officer or a van anywhere.

"Hey," shouted a breathless voice from behind me.

I turned around. It was Mei-Li. She had obviously run all the way from school because her face looked like someone had thrown a wet towel at it.

"What—did you—say to the police?" she demanded, gripping her stomach. "You didn't tell them it was Thomas, did you?"

I gave her a scowl. "What's it to you if I did or didn't?"

Mei-Li shook her head. "You're—you're so—*stupid*! You KNOW it wasn't him."

"He was lying," I argued back. "I know what I saw."

Mei-Li clutched her sides even tighter, just like I did whenever we had to run too many circles in PE. Then, without saying another word, she bolted off toward the lake.

Realizing what she was planning on doing, I raced after her, both of us reaching the army of oak trees at the exact same time. Thomas was there in the very same place we had left him yesterday, sitting outside his tent and reading a book that was nearly as old and as brown as him.

"Thomas!" cried Mei-Li as we both ran up to him.

He looked up at us, his bushy eyebrows separating like two hairy caterpillars crawling away from each other.

"Hello," he said, with a smile followed by a frown. The smile was for Mei-Li. The frown and the soft growling sound that came with it was for me. "Everything OK?"

Mei-Li shook her head and pointed at me. "HE'S told the police that YOU'RE the Invisible Thief and they're going to come after you and arrest you and make you go to jail, so you *have* to get away from here!"

"What?" asked Thomas, dropping his book. Three more long creases appeared on his forehead. "Why would you do that?"

"Because I told you, I *saw* you," I said, feeling triumphant. "You were lying down in a doorway and I was at the bus stop opposite. You didn't see me, but I saw you. I saw everything you did! You held up some remote-control thing to turn off all the lights, and then you climbed the fountain and sawed off the statue."

"I've already told you that wasn't me— Wait, you *really* saw one of the robberies?" asked the old man, his eyes widening so much that they made the bags under his eyes half disappear. "You saw the thief?"

"Yes, I saw YOU," I repeated.

"Look, you little menace," said Thomas, getting to his feet and hurriedly packing everything into a huge black rucksack that was almost as tall as I was. "I don't know *who* you saw, but it wasn't me, and it wasn't anyone who's ever been homeless. None of us who've lived on the streets would spray our code around the way this thief is doing. And you're more stupid than I took you for if you think any of us have the tools to steal a banana from a fruit farm, let alone public pieces of art!" Stopping his packing for a moment, the old man looked at me from my shoes to my eyes, and added, "But then again, maybe you are more stupid than you look."

"You're just mad because I figured it out," I shouted.

Hoisting his bag on to his shoulder, the old man looked down at me and whispered, "You figured out wrong, boy."

"I'm so sorry, Thomas," said Mei-Li, who was looking as if she was about to cry. "It's all my fault. I should never have brought *him* here."

"Ah, not to worry, my girl," said the old man as he tapped

her gently on the cheek. "Should think I'd be used to it by now. Anything that goes wrong anywhere, somehow it's got to be our fault. You tell your dad to let everyone know there's a spot going for a while," he added, nodding at the tent.

"WAIT," I said, trying to think of some way of keeping him in the park. If he left and the police couldn't find him, no one would know it was me who had caught him! "The police are already on their way—if you run now, it'll just make things worse for you."

"I'll take my chances, thanks," replied Thomas as he tucked his wallet safely away in his coat. "You tell your mates in the police good luck for me, and in the meantime, I'd advise you to get your eyes tested."

As he walked away, Mei-Li gave me a look—a look that told me that as much as she had hated me before, she hated me a million times more now. But I wasn't ready for when she stepped forward and, with a loud grunt that sounded like a scream cut short, pushed me to the ground.

I stared up at her, too shocked to say anything. And before I could get back up, she had run out of the trees and vanished into the same blinding tunnel of sunlight the old man had walked into.

I got up and hurried out of the trees to follow them. But they had both disappeared into the crowds of dogs and people and joggers and cyclists, and I had no idea which way they had gone. The park was too big and had too many exit gates. There was nothing I could do, so I walked home, hating Mei-Li for ruining everything for me.

"Hectoooooooor! Is that you?" shrieked my mum as soon as I opened the front door. She was hovering in the corridor like a traffic warden waiting to give someone a parking ticket.

I wanted to ask her who else she thought it was going to be, but I could tell right away that wouldn't be a good idea. She looked angry.

Helen poked her head out of the living room and watched from a safe distance.

"Hector, maybe you can tell me why I got a call today, right in the middle of an important meeting, with the news that MY son was being interviewed by the police! The POLICE!"

I stood quietly and waited. If you interrupted Mum when she was shouting at you, it made her go on for longer.

"I cannot *believe* that you would come up with a story about seeing a crime and then lie to the police about it! Do you know how serious that is?"

"*I* didn't," I said, slipping past her and running up the stairs. "I didn't lie!"

"You get back here RIGHT NOW!" shouted Mum, ignoring what I had just said. She was angry, but not angry enough to follow me up the stairs. "You wait until your dad gets home, young man. This is the last straw! I'm sick to the back teeth of having to try and make excuses for you and always worrying about what trouble you'll be getting into next!"

I slammed my bedroom door shut and chucked my rucksack on to the floor. But straightaway, I heard footsteps outside and then a loud annoying knock. Before I could even answer it, my door swung open, making me wish for the millionth time that I was allowed to have a lock on it.

It was Helen, looking redder and spottier than ever. "Go away," I warned.

"Did you *really* tell the police you saw the thief?" she asked.

"Yeah," I said. "So?"

"You *do* know that you can get locked up in prison for lying to the police, right?" she said, putting her hands on her hips. "It's called obstruction of justice."

"I'm NOT lying," I said, pushing her out of my room and closing the door in her face. "YOU'LL SEE!"

"Yeah, well, don't expect me to help you if you are," shouted Helen through the door.

"LIKE YOU EVER WOULD," I shouted back. I could hear her footsteps as she stomped downstairs.

My stomach was growling at me, so I pulled out my stash box and, sitting down at my desk, started to munch on an extra-large chocolate nut bar and a bag of onion rings. As I switched on my computer and poured the last crumbs of the chips straight into my mouth, my bedroom door swung open again. I got ready to yell at Helen to get out, but it was only Hercules. He was playing his favorite game of pretending to be jumping on an imaginary pogo stick. For some reason, he had a line of glitter joining up his eyebrows.

"Boing-boing-boing," he announced, bouncing in a circle around me. "Hup-tor, look! This is an extra boing!" And climbing up on to my bed, he began to jump up and down on my pillows.

"Stop it," I said, feeling annoyed. "Get down and go away."

"Boing-boing-boing," he replied, jumping higher.

I stretched out my hand and pushed Hercules away. But I pushed him harder than I meant to, and instead of landing safely on the floor, he fell sideways off the bed and bumped his head against my wardrobe.

He turned red and began to cry loudly, sticking his fingers in his mouth—something he only did when he was really hurt.

"Shhh!" I said. "I'm sorry, Hercules. Are you OK?" I rubbed his arms the way Lisa did when he fell.

"You pushed meeeeeeeee," wailed Hercules, still crying.

"I didn't mean to," I said, listening for the sound of Lisa or Mum running up the stairs. "Look," I went on, pulling out my stash box. "You can take anything you want, OK? But you HAVE to stop crying."

Sucking on his fingers extra hard for a few seconds,

Hercules gulped down his tears as I checked his head. There was a tiny bump rising out of the side of it like a bread roll. I promised myself that if it went down quickly and I didn't get caught, I wouldn't push Hercules ever again.

"Can I have this one?" he asked, looking at me with his watery eyes and pointing to the only remaining caramel-covered chocolate nut bar—something that I would never normally have given him.

"Sure," I said, ripping it open for him.

Hercules took the chocolate bar and a handful of other sweets and, climbing back up on to my bed, began chomping his way through everything as if nothing had ever happened. I turned to my computer, feeling thankful that Dad had given me the new password for doing such a good job at Mrs. Sanders's house—even though I hadn't spent more than half an hour with her. All she had wanted was for me to dig up some weeds—which I had done so super fast that even I couldn't believe it. I pulled on my headphones to drown out the sounds of rustling bags and Hercules munching like a hamster and got ready to find out what the signs the thief had used meant. Dad had said you could only understand them if you knew the secret code, but I was sure the code would be online somewhere.

As I clicked on the search bar on the top of my screen, Hercules called out, "Look, Hup-tor!" Putting dots of melted chocolate all over his face and nose with his pudgy finger, he explained, "I'm Helen!"

I gave him a grin and said, "You look just like her. You should go and show her, right now."

But he shook his head and, climbing down from the bed, came and stood next to me to make car noises instead. I typed in "homeless thief yellow signs," and we watched together as various images flooded the screen. There were the three diagonal lines that I had seen being sprayed on the fountain at Piccadilly Circus, the large circle that had been left at Sell-Fridges, a sign that looked like the head of a spear that had been sprayed at Paddington Station, and the drawing of a posh hat that had been left at the feet of the Peter Pan statue. None of the descriptions under the pictures said anything about what they were supposed to mean.

As I zoomed out of the image of the Peter Pan statue, Hercules giggled, and pointed at my computer, whispering, "Toilet."

"Don't be silly," I told him. "That's not a toilet."

Hercules pointed at it again, saying, "Yes it is! I know how to spell it now, Lisa taught me. T-O-Y-L-E-T!"

I leaned forward to see what he was pointing at. It was a sign shaped like a white flag hanging on the building next to the Peter Pan hospital, which said "TO LET" in giant red letters. Above the giant red letters was a symbol of two bright blue dragons breathing fire, standing on either side of the words "Lordship London Properties."

"It doesn't say 'toilet,'" I explained. "It says 'To Let.' It's just a sign for people who want to rent a space out."

But Hercules had toilets on the brain, and as I scrolled through more pictures about the robberies, he shouted "TOY-LETS" at all of them. Then he got bored and ran back downstairs to show Helen the chocolate version of her face.

Even after Hercules left and I could concentrate again, I couldn't find any information about what the coded messages meant. So, giving up, I switched over to my game and began taking over just as many universes as I could instead.

The Boy Who Cried "Mistake!"

FOR THE NEXT FEW DAYS, RIGHT UP UNTIL THE WEEKEND, ALL THE whole school could talk about was me and how I had seen the thief.

Even Randy and Lavinia and kids I usually went after began to boast that I had told them things while taking their sweets and chips and money. But the truth was, no one knew anything, because I hadn't told anyone anything. Not even Will and Katie. The stories seemed to be growing all by themselves, like invisible seeds watered by invisible words.

By dismissal on Friday afternoon, without me even saying a thing, I had become a skateboarding champion who had chased down the Invisible Thief all on my own, right after Will had nearly broken his leg doing a triple bar jump.

The only person who didn't seem to care was Mei-Li. So I tried my best to *make* her care. I tripped her up and called her names and laughed at her weird lunches and even got Will and Katie to accidentally-on-purpose spill a bottle of extra-sticky, extra-shaken fizzy orangeade all over her. We all got a week's worth of detention for everything, but she still pretended I didn't exist.

"We need to come up with something better for her," remarked Katie as we headed home on Friday after the first of multiple detentions Mr. Lancaster had given us for the orangeade bottle trick. "She's acting like she's not scared of us at all. It's weird."

"Let's think of something good over the weekend," said Will. "Hey, you guys want to go boarding at Piccadilly Circus tomorrow? In case the thief comes back?"

"They won't be there again, stupid," said Katie, sneering. "Nobody steals from the same place twice. Look at all the different places they've stolen from just this week. They stole stuff from that square named after the cheese—"

"Leicester cheese," grinned Will. "My favorite."

"Right," said Katie, rolling her eyes. "They stole Charlie Chaplin's stick, and Mary Poppins's umbrella, and the *other* Paddington Bear's sandwich from there. But then, after that, they stole those lamps from the front doors of the place where the Queen buys all her food from—"

"Fortress and Mason's," interrupted Will, knowingly.

"It's Fort*num* and Mason," corrected Katie, shaking her head. "I mean, none of it makes sense, does it? But one thing they're definitely *not* doing is going back to somewhere they've stolen from before."

"But all the places are still in the same part of London, though, aren't they?" pointed out Will. "That Fortnum place was only down the road from the fountain. So you never know!"

Will looked over at me as if asking me to back him up. I felt sorry for him, because I knew he was desperate to get interviewed by the police and become as famous as me. So I gave him an "I guess."

As we reached the corner shop, we slowed down to see if there was anyone with anything we wanted. But only a few people were around, and Mr. McEwan was watching us, so we carried on walking.

"Want to come to the park tomorrow?" asked Katie. "My brother said he's going to get me one of those new Frisbees that makes a noise when you throw it."

Will shrugged. "Maybe."

"Can't," I said. I didn't want to tell them that I was going to the police station just yet. I wanted to surprise them with the news after Thomas had been caught and I was in the papers proving everyone wrong. Mum had said the police wanted to record me properly and take a statement, which meant she was finally taking me seriously too. "I'm still grounded," I said, because technically, I still was.

"That's rubbish," said Katie.

"Yeah," I agreed, thinking about how exciting it was going to be to make an official statement and be listened to properly for once. "Totally rubbish."

My interview at the police station didn't go exactly as I had expected.

First of all, a man called Inspector Wyde—whose face was so wide that my face could have fit into his at least twice—took me and Mum into a waiting room. He told me that hundreds of people were ringing to say they knew something about the thief.

"However," he said, eyeing me carefully, "so far, your story is the only one that has checked out. So we'll put it on record, if that's OK with you."

I hadn't realized I was in competition with hundreds of people, and it put me in a bad mood. After Inspector Wyde had finished talking, Officer Miriam and a man called Mr. Riddles, who he said was a sketch artist, came and took me and Mum into a small gray room. They asked me to tell my story again and again and describe everything I saw, just like Mr. Lancaster did sometimes when he wanted to check I was telling the truth.

They made me answer so many questions about what I had and hadn't seen and what bus me and Will had taken and what had happened at exactly what time and if I was *sure* it was Thomas from the park, that I started wishing I hadn't said anything to anyone at all.

"I've already told you all this," I moaned. "His name is Thomas and he lives in the park. And sometimes outside the McEwans' shop. It was him."

"It doesn't hurt to be sure," said Officer Miriam, smiling.

"Doesn't hurt you," I muttered, kicking the table leg hard enough to make a sound, but not so hard that it shook anything.

"OK. Last thing," said Officer Miriam. "Can you describe exactly what the man you saw at Piccadilly Circus looked like? We want you to tell us in as much detail as possible."

Taking a deep breath, I described what Thomas looked like, and Mr. Riddles asked me lots of questions about the shape of his nose and eyes and the bushiness of his eyebrows. As I talked, he drew quickly, making loud scratching noises on the white pad resting on his knees. Mr. Riddles had a big swirly mustache that was orange, and his glasses were orange too. He didn't look like someone who would work for the police.

"Was it a fluffy beard or a *curly* beard?" asked Mr. Riddles, for what must have been the seventh time.

"Both," I said. "Fluffy *and* curly."

"Like this?" Mr. Riddles held up the picture he had been drawing. Mr. Riddles had tried to draw Thomas from my description, but I had never described someone's face before so I didn't have enough words for exactly how he looked. But the drawing had Thomas's half-fluffy, half-curly beard, and his wrinkly old black coat collar, and his slightly bent nose, which I guessed were all the most important things.

When I nodded, Officer Miriam said thank you and told me I could go home. She also told Mum she would be in touch if anything happened.

But just like most grown-ups, she lied. Because by Sunday night, with no warning at all, Mr. Riddles's picture of Thomas the old man was on the nightly news, floating behind a reporter who was telling the world that the "Invisible Thief" had finally been spotted by "an Anonymous Source."

"Hectorrrrrrrrr! You're an Anonymous Source!" cried Lisa as Mum patted me on the back and told me she was proud of me and Hercules clapped without really knowing why. Helen didn't say anything and seemed to get even grumpier when Dad phoned from somewhere in Norway to tell me "Well done" and that I could pick one thing I wanted him to buy for me on account of me helping the police.

By Monday morning, the drawing was everywhere. I mean, *everywhere.* The police had used it to make giant "HAVE YOU SEEN THIS MAN?" posters and put them not just in the newspapers, but on big supermarket advertising boards and the side of buses and lampposts and special milk bottles. There was even a poster in Mr. and Mrs. McEwans's shopwindow and they *never* put anything in the shopwindow. Not even signs for lost puppies.

Will and Katie told everyone it had been me who had

described the thief to the police, and by the next day, I was being followed around and asked to sign copies of the poster for everyone.

But the more posters people brought for me to sign, and the more I had to look at the picture of the old man, the more I began to feel that something about it wasn't right. By Wednesday, I was starting to wonder if the police were playing a trick on me and had changed the picture somehow.

"Do you think the picture looks like the old trolley man?" I asked Will and Katie as I watched them adding horns and a red mustache to one of the posters outside school.

Katie stepped back and looked at the poster with her head to the side. "Yeah. If you look at it this way and pretend he's melting a bit."

"Sure," Will said. "Just, you know, older and uglier."

After we had drawn horns and snot balls and lizard tongues on three more posters and I had signed them too, I headed home, still wondering why the picture was bugging me.

As I opened the front door, my nose hoovered up a wonderful smell. It was my lucky day! Lisa's homemade fries made out of potatoes with the peel still on were the best thing on the planet to eat, even though she never made enough of them.

"What's that, Hercules?" I asked, chucking my bag in the corner of the kitchen. He was at the table, scribbling at something with his drawing pencils and glitter pens.

Hercules held up one of the Wanted posters with a proud

smile. He had covered it with glitter stars and colored the woolly hat bright green.

"Where did he get that?" I asked Lisa as she put down a large bowl of fries and chicken nuggets and a plate on the table in front of me.

"We got it from the lamppost outside, didn't we?" asked Lisa as she stroked Hercules's hair. "Now, eat quickly, please. Hercules has already had his food. Helen's got some friends coming around soon and they'll need the table."

I grunted. I hated all of Helen's friends. All they did was giggle and carry around fuzzy pencils and pretend they were doing homework together when really they were signing the names of their make-believe boyfriends in the backs of their books.

Smothering my mountain of fries and nuggets in ketchup so that it looked like an exploding volcano, I gulped it all down as Hercules busily colored in his poster. You could always tell when Hercules was being busy and serious because he hummed to himself and kicked the legs of his chair as if they were drums. He had just finished going over the eyes in bright blue pencil mixed with golden glitter and was now coloring in the beard in bright red crayon, even though he had colored the hair that was sticking out from under the hat in silver glitter.

I stopped chewing and gave an extra-loud gulp. I suddenly realized what was wrong with the poster and why it had been bugging me all day.

The man at the fountain had taken his hat off when he had bowed at the screens . . . and when he had, I'd seen the top of his head. It had shone a strange silvery color, just like Hercules's glitter. Which meant that his hair hadn't matched his beard, because his beard had been dark. But Thomas's hair *did* match his beard—they were *both* dark. I had seen it when he had gotten angry at me that day in the park and taken off his hat. Which meant . . . which meant . . .

The picture was wrong and right all at once!

"Poo!" cried Hercules as the crayon in his hand accidentally went outside the lines.

Mr. Riddles had drawn exactly what I described to him at the police station—but the face on the poster didn't look like Thomas's, because it hadn't been Thomas's face that I had been describing! It was another face. An old face that in some strange way looked familiar, but didn't look familiar at all at the same time . . .

I dropped the extra-large fry I had just picked up and pushed my chair away from the table. I wasn't hungry anymore, and I would probably never be hungry again. I had made the biggest mistake anyone on the planet could ever make—and no one could ever know.

The Kitchen of Soup

THE NEXT MORNING WAS SO GRAY AND WET AND WINDY, IT FELT AS IF winter had suddenly come back and was trying to make my mood even worse than it already was. I got wet on the way to school because the zip on my coat was broken and I couldn't find my hoodie anywhere. And once I got to the playground, Mr. Lancaster was shouting at everyone to head straight to class even though it wasn't first bell yet, so I couldn't get any extra snacks from anyone. The whole school seemed to shake and shiver with the wind and huge fat raindrops sploshed like cannonballs onto the windows, dribbling down the glass and leaving behind wobbly slug trails.

The weather made everyone quieter than normal. Mrs. Vergara had said we could sit where we liked until the bell rang, but there wasn't much to do except talk. Or catch up with homework like Rania and Joseph were doing, but nobody else was sad enough to do that. Not even Mei-Li. I could see her playing some sort of puzzle game with Robert and giggling.

"I think I might die if I get any more bored," said Katie, holding up her chin with her hands. Will and me were sitting at her table. "Do you think that's possible?" Not waiting for a reply, she added, "Lavinia and that new boy were meant to bring me gobstoppers as well. . . . I'll have to try and get them at lunchtime."

Will nodded, but I wasn't really listening. I was looking at the front of the class, where Robert and Mei-Li were sitting.

"What do you think, H?" asked Will, thumping me on the arm.

"Huh?"

"Can you believe they got seventy-two?"

"Seventy-two what?" I asked. "Gobstoppers?"

"No." Will looked at Katie, who was shaking her head at me.

"Homeless people," said Will. "The police arrested seventy-two homeless men yesterday."

"What?" I asked, feeling a bit sick.

"Because of your poster," said Katie, moving her glasses up and down from behind her ears. "Hey, imagine them all standing in a line looking the same. That would be so funny!"

I opened my mouth to ask if they were sure but was interrupted by the bell ringing and Mrs. Vergara telling everyone to return to their seats. I got up and went to my table, where Rajesh was waiting for me to give him his secret morning punch. But I couldn't be bothered today. All I wanted was to get home and go to bed and make my head stop thumping.

I waited for the day to finish, but it wouldn't. In fact, it dragged on and on, and the rain and the wind and the low gray clouds made each lesson feel like forever. Mrs. Vergara tried to make things fun by putting on some music during break and reading a funny book at lunchtime, but she seemed to be boring even herself and in the end she gave up.

The darker and wetter the day and the skies got, the more I couldn't stop thinking about the poster and the seventy-two old homeless men Katie had imagined standing in a row. Maybe it didn't matter if I had got it wrong. I'd given them the right description after all, just the wrong name. Maybe one of the seventy-two men they'd arrested *was* the man I'd seen. And if none of them were the thief, then they probably knew who it was or would at least know what the signs meant. Besides, people on TV were always talking about how home-less people were "stains" on the community—as if they were blobs of dirt in those TV ads for fabric softener. Those seventy-two men had probably been up to no good anyway. I had done everyone a favor by getting them arrested and off the streets.

But if that was true, then why had my stomach started thumping as much as my head? Why was I worried if Thomas had been caught and put in jail in place of the real thief with the silvery hair? Why did I care if, because of me, lots of homeless people were arrested instead of the real thief? It didn't matter!

Except I knew it did. Because if the truth came out, the police and Mei-Li and Mum and Dad and Helen and Mr. Lancaster and Mrs. Vergara and the McEwans and the whole school would think I was a coward and liar and had tried to get Thomas into trouble on purpose. They would never believe anything I ever said or did again, and maybe the police would want to arrest me for obstructing justice, just like Helen had warned. . . . I had to find out the truth, and there was only one person who could help me. Except she now hated me even more than I hated her, and even though I kept looking at her in class all day, she didn't look back at me even once.

"Make sure you all wrap up warm now," said Mrs. Vergara as the bell for home time finally rang, and everyone hopped out of their seats like kangaroos. "I don't want any sniffling in class tomorrow."

Katie and Will didn't bother putting on their coats. It was only Thursday, which meant we still had two more days of detention left to do with Mr. Lancaster for picking on Mei-Li.

"Aren't you coming?" asked Will as I pulled on my coat.

I shook my head. "Can't. Headache," I said, and ran out into the corridor. I had to speak to Mei-Li—even if it meant

Mr. Lancaster giving me an extra three detentions for missing this one.

I saw Mei-Li walking with Rania and Robert and Joshua out of the school gates and, bowing my head low against the pelting rain, followed them out of the playground from a distance. Robert and Joshua stopped at the McEwans' shop, which left just Mei-Li and Rania walking toward the park. I worried that Rania wasn't going to leave her, but then at the end of the road she turned right, and Mei-Li waved and turned left.

I sped up, wondering why Mei-Li was taking the long way around the park instead of going through it like she usually did. She walked past the first entrance and then the second. Suddenly she began to run, so I began to run too. I had nearly caught up with her when, just as suddenly as she had started, she stopped, making me nearly crash into her.

She turned around. "Why are you following me?" she asked, looking out from under the pointy hood of her bright yellow raincoat. She had tied it so tightly around her face that she looked like a squashed lemon.

"I need to talk to you," I said. My voice was shaking from the cold. "About the poster . . . and T-Thomas. I . . . I think I made a mistake."

Mei-Li stared at me. I was so wet and cold that I couldn't even feel my face anymore.

"Leave me alone," she said.

Before I could respond, she turned around and hurried down the road, turning right at a crossing just before the high street. I ran after her in time to see her walk straight up to the doors of a big redbrick building, which had a banner that said "SOUP KITCHEN, EVERYONE WELCOME" above it.

Groaning out loud, I forced myself to follow her in. Walking through the huge wooden doors, I entered a hall full of tables and chairs and people in coats chatting and drinking tea from paper cups. The room smelled of wet dog and tangy old fruit so much that I felt as if I could taste it. I pinched my nose closed and scanned the room for Mei-Li. I spotted her heading to the back of the hall, waving at people as she walked by.

"Ah, it's a good day when Mei-Li's around," called out a man in a bright purple coat, giving her a thumbs up.

Mei-Li gave him one back, but she didn't stop.

"Mei-Li!" I cried out. She ignored me and kept walking.

"Hey, Mei-Li, tell your dad to put some spice in the food," joked a woman with wild blond hair who was holding a cup of tea. Her eyes looked both young and old at the same time, and she was carrying a big plastic bag on her arm that was so muddy and tattered it looked as if it had just been dug out of the ground.

"Will do," said Mei-Li, still moving.

"Hey, Mei-Li—stop!" I yelled, pushing past everyone to try and get to her.

"Mei-Li, got any of my favorite cookies today?" asked a man with huge brown ropes of twisted hair.

"I'll ask, I promise," shouted back Mei-Li.

By now, we had reached the back of the hall, where a big silver kitchen lay on the other side of a huge stainless-steel counter. It was filled with people wearing blue plastic gloves and black T-shirts that said "Lotus Soup Kitchen." They were all making teas and chopping things and moving around each other as if they were in a dance.

"Mei-Li, you're late, darling," said a tall man who was unwrapping big blocks of butter. He was dressed in one of the black T-shirts, with faded blue jeans. He had the same black hair as Mei-Li's. Except his was short and spiky. And he had the exact same face shape too.

"Some volunteers haven't shown up, so we're short today," he continued as he dropped a kiss on the top of her head.

"Sorry, Phay-Phay," said Mei-Li, taking off her coat, still ignoring me completely.

"Hey, who's this?" asked the man, noticing me.

"I'm a friend," I cut in, before Mei-Li could say anything. "I've come to . . . to help out," I added. I looked over at Mei-Li, but she was looking straight ahead.

"It's very nice of you to volunteer with us," the man said. "I'm Mei-Li's dad, Cheng. I always like meeting my daughter's new school friends. What's your name?"

"Kevin," answered Mei-Li quickly.

I gave her a frown, but she continued to look straight ahead at her dad.

Mr. Cheng smiled at us both, not seeming to notice anything strange. "Well, Kevin, you're very wet, eh? But your arms look strong! How about you both get washed up and take over the cheese grating duties? We've got a few hundred potatoes, all in need of mountains of cheese."

Before I could say that actually I had changed my mind, a woman handed me a plastic apron and some gloves and pushed me to the middle of the kitchen.

"Come on, then," challenged Mei-Li, glaring at me hard. "Since you've come to help out. Or are you too chicken?"

"No," I said, following her to the sink. Copying everything she did, I washed my hands and put on the apron and the gloves, and then went and stood next to her at a big metal table. A huge man who could easily have played a giant in any play with a giant in it placed the largest block of cheese I had ever seen in front of me and chuckled, "Good luck, newbie!"

"Hurry up," ordered Mei-Li as she began to grate her block of cheese. Every few minutes she would pause to put large handfuls of the cheese on to the rows of steaming hot potatoes that were quickly being placed in front of us.

Not wanting to be beaten by her, I grated as fast as I could. The kitchen was full of the noises of people cooking— microwaves pinging and ovens whirring and pans of water boiling and bubbling. There were lots of things being

141

made—not just baked potatoes. One woman was filling containers with rice and kidney beans in some sort of red sauce, and handing them out to people who were licking their lips and smiling. The color of the sauce reminded me of the things Mei-Li brought in her packed lunches and made me wonder if, instead of teasing her about them and throwing them in the trash can, maybe I should have tried them. If what she had was even half as good as the bright red bean dish smelled, I would eat it all the time too.

Peeking out into the hall, I could see that it was even busier now. It was packed with people who were all just as smelly and as weird-looking as each other. Some of them were sitting and talking to people in the Lotus Soup Kitchen T-shirts, holding their hands and nodding. Some were playing chess or cards or other board games. Right at the back of the hall was a woman surrounded by piles of old clothes, who was helping people find pieces that might fit them. And next to her was a man standing at a table covered with cans of food and bags of bread that he was giving out to people. There wasn't a single bag of chips or any chocolate bars on that table, which made me wonder what happened if anyone ever wanted a treat and not a loaf of bread or can of baked beans.

My arms began to get sore from the grating, so I slowed down and looked around the room again. A young woman who looked better dressed and cleaner than everyone else was walking through the hall. Her face and eyes were red, and right behind her were two small children who looked wet and miserable. Coming up to the kitchen counter, she waved at Mr. Cheng.

"Hi, Cheng. Have you got anything for the kids by any chance?" she asked quietly.

"Always," he said, going to the back of the kitchen and pulling out two large bags from underneath a bench. I could see they were filled with sweets and chips and toys. The children clapped their hands and immediately started looking through them as the woman started to cry.

"Now, now," said Mr. Cheng, leaving the kitchen to give her a hug. "Why don't you tell me what's happening with those bailiffs of yours." Leading her to the back of the hall, he went and sat down with her at an empty table.

"Why was that woman crying?" I asked Mei-Li as I tried to catch up with her cheese grating. She was stronger and faster than she looked.

Mei-Li shrugged as if she didn't want to answer me. But then she said, "Her husband keeps gambling, so they never have enough money for food and he's not very nice to her. That's why she comes here with her children. Sometimes the food she gets here is the only food they have all day, and my dad and everyone are trying to stop her from losing her house."

"Oh," I said.

"Come on kids, chop, chop. Just a hundred more portions

to go! It's busy to-niiiiiight," sung the giant man as he put another big block of cheese next to me. I began wondering why soup kitchens were called soup kitchens when there didn't seem to be a single bowl of soup anywhere.

By the time all the potatoes had cheese on them and they had been handed out to the people in the hall, my arms were numb and I was so tired that I felt as if I had run at least thirteen marathons.

"Well done, Kevin," said Mr. Cheng. He handed me and Mei-Li a large cookie and a glass of milk each. "Here you go. For your brilliant efforts."

I stared down at the cookie and the glass of milk. "Wait a minute," I said, looking at Mei-Li. "You don't even get paid? You just get a cookie?"

"No one here gets paid!" Mei-Li said, rolling her eyes. "Everyone's a volunteer."

I looked around at the giant man and the old woman who were now putting hot cookies on big plates, and the two young men who were dancing to the radio while scrubbing the cooker, and decided all of them were mad.

Mei-Li went to a bench at the back of the kitchen and sat down. I followed her and watched as she took a big bite of her cookie and a gulp of her milk.

"Why did you tell your dad my name was Kevin?" I asked, sitting a little bit farther down the bench.

"Because if he knew who you really were, he'd have made you leave," said Mei-Li.

144

I could feel myself turn bright red.

"You mean, you tell him . . . ?"

Mei-Li nodded. "I have to when I come home covered in orangeade and with scabby knees and stuff."

I turned the cookie over in my hand. I hadn't thought about anyone going home and telling their parents what I had done to them. My parents never asked me anything about school unless I had got into trouble, so I'd thought it was the same for everyone else.

"Oh," I said, not really knowing what to do next.

We sat in silence for a few seconds, before, finally, Mei-Li spoke.

"What do you want? Why did you follow me here?" she asked.

"I told you. I think I made a mistake. I think I gave the police the wrong name. So I need to find him. Thomas, I mean. And I wanted to know if you knew where he is."

Mei-Li shook her head. "No one's seen him since that day he left the park. You know, when he found out you'd LIED to the police about him."

"I wasn't lying," I argued, wanting her to know that I wasn't a liar. "Not on purpose anyway. I thought it was Thomas—the thief looked *exactly* like him. I promise! But then yesterday I remembered—the man I saw took off his hat and bowed in front of the big lights. And when he did that, he had silvery hair on top of his head—not dark brown like Thomas's hair."

I looked at Mei-Li and waited to see if she believed me.

Her eyes were narrowed, and she was biting her bottom lip so much it had disappeared into her mouth.

"So what do you want to do?" she asked finally. "Go and tell the police you made a mistake?"

I shook my head. "I can't. They'll probably think I obstructed their justice on purpose and arrest me."

"Yeah," she said. "Probably."

I swallowed the milk as slowly as I could, waiting for her to say something else. Just as I reached the point where there wasn't anything left to gulp, Mei-Li nodded.

"OK," she said slowly. "I'll help you, but only because I want the police to know it wasn't Thomas. Or any of them," she added, nodding toward all the homeless people in the hall.

I was so relieved that I released a small burp by accident. "Thanks," I said.

Mei-Li thought for another minute. Then she leaned forward.

"We need to find Thomas," she said. "The only way we can prove he didn't do it is to catch the actual thief, and to do that, we need help."

She looked toward the front of the kitchen, where the giant man was handing out takeout boxes at the counter. "Solo, is Catwoman here today?" she called out.

The man looked around the hall, slowly revolving left to right like a lighthouse. He shook his head. "Nah, my plum. She's not here today. Probably visiting her friends. But she'll be here on Saturday. You know she never misses Saturday lunch."

"Thanks, Solo." Looking back at me, Mei-Li asked, "Can you be here on Saturday at twelve o'clock?"

"Yeah," I said. "Why?"

"Because I think I've got a plan," said Mei-Li. "But first we need to talk to Catwoman."

Catwoman and the Fortnum's Mason

AFTER SPENDING ALL OF FRIDAY TRYING TO CATCH UP WITH MR. LAN-caster's detentions and keeping Katie and Will away from Mei-Li so that they wouldn't ever guess she was trying to help me, I couldn't wait for Saturday to arrive. When it finally did, I woke up feeling as though I had at least thirty Ping-Pong balls bouncing around inside me. I got out of bed much earlier than usual. I couldn't wait to find out who Catwoman was and what she had to do with finding Thomas. Since I didn't know anything about Mei-Li's plan, I had spent all my time in detention drawing out my own plan. It probably wasn't going to be half as good as Mei-Li's plan because she knew everyone who Thomas knew and I didn't. But then, her plan probably didn't involve cool things like getting dressed up in capes and learning how to hot wire a car by tonight like mine did.

"Hey, look who's up with the birds for once," said Dad,

glancing over his newspaper at me as I walked into the kitchen. He had flown back from Norway the night before and had obviously spent all night working. He was still in yesterday's clothes and was sitting alone, drinking a cup of coffee that was so strong it made the whole kitchen smell like a compost heap that had been set on fire. I had forgotten him and Mum were going to be home all weekend.

"What are you up to today?" he asked. He was frowning at me. He was always frowning at me, even when I hadn't done anything.

"Nothing," I said, not looking at him as I went to the fridge and got out the milk bottle. It had one of my Wanted posters on it staring out at me. So I put it back and got out the orange juice instead.

"Come on. That can't be the case. When I was your age, I was busier at home than I was at school! Books . . . games . . . radio shows . . . homework . . . weekend clubs . . . barely had time for any of it," said Dad.

"Sorry I wasn't born in the eighteen hundreds," I muttered, wondering why parents always talked about what they did when they were kids whenever they wanted to point out what you *weren't* doing. It wasn't our fault they didn't have computer games or probably even television when they were small. And anyway, there weren't any clubs to join around here. Not unless you liked wearing tights and making an idiot of yourself on a stage or playing boring soccer. There weren't any games clubs or skateboarding clubs to join. Not in this uncool part of London anyway.

Dad chuckled at what I'd said and went back to reading his paper. I watched him for a second. I knew I was still technically grounded for staying out so late that Saturday night in Piccadilly Circus, even though Dad had bought me the big holographic skull sticker I wanted for my skateboard for helping the police. But until today, it hadn't really mattered if I had been grounded or not, because Mum and Dad hadn't been around. Now they were home, I realized I would have to find some way of getting out of the house to go and see Mei-Li.

Maybe it was a good thing I had woken up so early. This was the best time to try and get Dad on my side—he was always easier to convince than Mum.

"Dad?"

"Hmmmm?"

"Am I still grounded?"

"Yup."

"Even though I'm helping the police now?"

"Yup."

"Oh. It's just . . . I told a friend from school that I would help them at a soup kitchen today, at lunchtime."

If I had said I was planning to run down the street without any pants on, throwing chocolate eggs at everyone, I think Dad would have had a calmer reaction. He spluttered on his coffee, dropped his newspaper, and then dropped his jaw too—so wide I could see nearly all his fillings.

"A soup kitchen? *You?*"

"Yeah!" I said, getting ready for him to laugh at me.

"YOU?" asked Dad, louder.

"Yeah," I repeated, scowling.

"Well . . . that's one for the books."

"What's one for the books, Dad?" asked Helen, half skipping her way into the kitchen and throwing her arms around his neck.

"Your brother there," said Dad, pointing at me as if she didn't know who I was, "says he's helping at a soup kitchen today."

"As if!" smirked Helen.

"I am!" I snapped. "At twelve o'clock!"

"Which one, then?" tested Helen.

"The Lotus Soup Kitchen," I said, lifting my chin. "In the church off the high street."

My dad pushed his glasses up as if he wanted to see me properly now. "You mean the one run by Mr. Zhou—Mr. Cheng Zhou?"

So Mei-Li had been right. Her dad and my dad *did* know each other.

"Yeah. His daughter Mei-Li's in my class," I said.

"Well, that's . . . fantastic," said Dad, still sounding as if he couldn't quite believe it. "I haven't seen the place myself yet, but I keep meaning to stop by. How about I drive you there at eleven-thirty?"

"OK." I shrugged, trying to make it seem as if it was no big deal. Even though this was the first time in years Dad had offered to take me anywhere.

"I've been meaning to see if it's the kind of place I'm after for the film. And I need to drop your sister off for her violin lesson too. Three birds, one stone," said Dad, winking at me.

I took my orange juice and sneaked half a pack of cookies back up to my room. I didn't know how I felt about being a bird my dad wanted to throw a stone at.

At exactly half past eleven, I grabbed my skateboard and rucksack, which was packed with as many snacks from my stash box as I could fit into it, and headed down to the front door. Everyone was waiting in the corridor as if I was leaving for the airport and might never come back again.

"I want to goooo," moaned Hercules.

"Not today darling," said Mum. "Hector, I think it's brilliant you're doing this. But you—you will behave, won't you?"

"Yeah," I said. What did she think I was going to do, nick the grated cheese?

When I got to the car, Helen was already in the front seat, with her arms wrapped around her violin case.

After beeping through Saturday-morning traffic, Dad pulled up to the soup kitchen and its big white sign.

"Helen, stay here," he said, unclipping his seatbelt. "I'm just going to go in and say hi to Mr. Zhou and his team."

That's when I remembered. Mei-Li's dad and his whole team thought my name was Kevin!

"NO," I shouted. "YOU CAN'T!"

"Why not?" asked Dad, turning to face me.

"Er . . . he won't have time to talk—Saturday's their busiest day," I said. "He said so. He said he would be rushed off his feet and not have time to talk to anyone at all."

I watched Dad as he thought about what I had said. "All right," he said, pulling his seatbelt back on. "I'll ring him next week instead. Come home straight after you're done, OK?"

I nodded and jumped out of the car, slamming the door shut before Dad could change his mind. Giving Helen a smile that I knew would torture her all day long, I sprinted in through the church doors.

Inside the hall, some of the volunteers were already helping groups of homeless people find chairs or get clothes. Today, there was also a new sign by a table that said "CLEANING STATION: GET YOUR SHOWER TOKEN HERE," where lots of the homeless people were queuing up. I could still smell everyone, but it didn't seem as bad as it had two days ago. Maybe my senses were being killed off.

"Kevin! You're back again," said Mr. Cheng with a smile. His arms were full of big towels and a pile of bright yellow soap bars. "Mei-Li's in the kitchen. Go and join her if you want."

I nodded and headed to the kitchen, where big puffs of smoke and steam were hissing into the air as if being released by a dragon's nostrils. The room was filled with far more people than on Thursday, so I had to push my way past everyone to get to Mei-Li. She was at the big metal table again, this time chopping up a big crate of cucumbers next to two other women.

She waved at me with her blue-gloved hands. "Catwoman should be here soon," she whispered. "But here, first put this on and come and help."

She took out a black T-shirt from the big pocket in her apron and held it out to me.

I shook my head. "I've only been here once before. I don't need a T-shirt."

"Dad wanted you to have it," said Mei-Li.

As I pulled it on, giant Solo shouted from across the kitchen, "HEY, LOOK EVERYONE! NEWBIE KEVIN'S ONE OF US NOW!" Pointing at me and making a trumpet noise, he started a clap for me that spread through the whole kitchen.

My face turned as red as the huge crate of red peppers in front of me, and I was sure there was steam coming out from the top of my hair. I quickly started chopping the nearest cucumber as fast as I could, not looking at anyone.

"Don't be embarrassed," said Mei-Li, grinning and chopping too. "They do that with everyone who's new."

"HEY, SWEET PLUM!" cried Solo to Mei-Li just as I had begun chopping my tenth cucumber. "CATWOMAN'S HEEEEERE! BY THE TINS."

Dropping her knife, Mei-Li ripped off her gloves and grabbed my arm. "Come on!" she said.

Ripping my gloves off too, I followed her out into the hall. Pushing our way to the back of it, we reached the big table of canned food, where a whole group of people were picking and choosing things to take.

I looked around for a woman carrying a cat or maybe wearing a cat T-shirt or even a Catwoman costume. Instead, Mei-Li walked up to an old woman with black curly hair and bright purple gloves with no fingers to them.

It was the same woman I had spoken to behind the station! The crazy one who had shouted at me!

Before I could warn her, Mei-Li tapped the woman on the arm. "Hi, Catwoman," she said.

"Oh, hello, darling," smiled the Catwoman, giving Mei-Li's cheek a tap. "You couldn't help me, could you love? I need some food for my babies."

"Wait here, I'll get it for you," said Mei-Li, signaling at me to stay where I was, before disappearing.

I stood next to the Catwoman but didn't look at her. I looked at the ceiling and then at the floor. But I could tell she was looking straight at me.

"You new here?" she asked.

I nodded, looking over my shoulder.

"And you're one of Mei-Li's friends?"

I nodded again, and this time looked down at my shoes.

"She's never brought any of her friends here before,"

continued the Catwoman. "But why do I get the feeling I've seen you somewhere before?"

I shrugged and then, without meaning to, looked right into the Catwoman's eyes. "A-ha!" said the Catwoman, clicking her fingers. "*You're* the boy with the skateboard."

"Here you go," said Mei-Li, coming over carrying a plastic bag filled with cat food.

"What's *he* doing here?" the Catwoman asked Mei-Li, taking a step back from me. "He's one of the gang who likes to harass me and my babies!" Her voice was getting louder.

Mei-Li looked at me as if to make sure I wasn't. I shook my head.

"We can explain, Catwoman," said Mei-Li, looking at me with a glare as if she wasn't sure whether to believe me or not. "Please, let's go outside. We need your help."

"Here, Mason, come with me and help me and Mei-Li check this kid out," said the Catwoman, tapping the arm of a tall man who had been standing behind her with two cans of tuna fish in his hands. He was wearing an old brown tweed suit that was too big for him, a slightly dirty shirt, and a bright blue bow tie with scribbly writing all over it that almost matched the blue of his eyes. He looked a bit like Mr. Lancaster—if Mr. Lancaster hadn't had a shower in ages and had gray hair.

Nodding, the man named Mason followed the Catwoman, Mei-Li and me out through the main doors and on to the small, empty patch of grass outside.

"What's all this about?" asked the Catwoman, not taking her eyes off my face.

"We're trying to find Thomas," I said.

"And why's that? Maybe you want to turn him in to the police? Surprised they haven't found him already, thanks to that ruddy poster." The Catwoman's swirly brown-green eyes stared at me, making me think that all the cats I had seen her with might not be the only reason why she was called Cat-woman.

I shook my head. "No. I want to prove to the police it's *not* him."

Mason patted the Catwoman's arm soothingly. "Perhaps you had better explain a little more, dear boy?" His voice was so posh it made me wonder if it was even his.

I looked over at Mei-Li. Suddenly I couldn't speak. The words "I was wrong and I'm sorry about it" wouldn't come out.

So it was Mei-Li who explained about the thief with the silvery hair and what I had really seen that night, and how I had made a mistake when I had told the police it was Thomas and how I wanted to make it right.

"That's why we have to find Thomas. He *must* have an alibi for all the nights of the robberies, and he might know something about the yellow signs, which could help us catch the real thief—and then Hector can help identify him properly, and the police won't charge him with obstructing justice. He's your best friend, isn't he, Catwoman? Can you help us find him? Please?" she finished.

The Catwoman and Mason looked at each other and spoke to one another with their eyes. Whatever they said, it made Mason lean in to examine my face, like an army general inspecting a horse. After a few seconds, he stood back up and gave the Catwoman a sharp nod.

"Maybe we can," she said. "*If* you're serious about setting things right and helping us catch the real thief that is. We don't have time to waste."

"Helping *you* catch the real thief? Do you mean . . . that you're already trying to find him too?" I asked.

"Of course," said Mason, straightening his bow tie. "You didn't think we would all sit back and let this jumbo-tooting self-hooting disgrace of a thief go around blaming *us* for everything, did you? We have the best eyes and ears all across this city trying to find out who they are."

"But if the thief is homeless, how come you don't know who it is yet?" I asked.

The Catwoman and Mason both winced as if I had kicked them in the legs at the exact same time.

"That thief *isn't* homeless," said the Catwoman, shaking her head at me. "Think, boy! These crimes need serious equipment. A place to store the statues. Whoever the thief is, they're using our secret symbols to make people think it's the homeless community destroying public property—to make people hate us even more than they already do." She gave a bitter laugh. "And besides, do any of us look like we've got the time or the energy to go robbing statues when we don't even have food for our cats or houses to live in?"

"And where do you think we'd get the highfalutin gadgets we'd need to switch off lights and cameras whenever we fancy it?" added Mason. "Even my blessed Fortnum's doesn't sell trinkets like that!"

"Fortnum's?" I asked.

"Young people these days," said Mason, shaking his head. "No clue, have they, Catwoman? Fortnum and Mason—my very humble abode, sir." Mason suddenly gave an over-the-top bow. "Just so happens, that dastardly thief of yours stopped by the other night and took the two lanterns from its entrance doors—together with the stone arms that were holding them! Priceless, beautiful lanterns they were. Honoring Fortnum and his dear friend Mason for decades—now gone! And the worst of it is, they were taken while I was there, sleeping right around the corner."

"And you didn't see anything?" I asked, remembering how quiet and quick the thief had been.

Mason shook his head sadly. "Not a single thing," he said.

"So will you help us?" asked Mei-Li again. "Will you get in touch with Thomas and let him know that we want to help?"

The Catwoman nodded slowly. "OK. Tabby can have a look for Thomas later this afternoon, once she's had something to eat." She held up the bag of cat food. "Can't expect her to work on an empty stomach. I'm not making any promises, mind; it's up to Thomas. Come see me at my place later today, around four. Can you manage that?"

Mei-Li nodded, so I did too, wondering how a cat called Tabby was supposed to get a message to anyone, let alone to Thomas.

"Good. And there best be NO funny business," added the Catwoman, poking me hard in the shoulder with a finger. "Any hint of something fishy, and me and my cats will be all over you. Understand, trolley boy?"

Trolley boy? I stared at her, my jaw as wide open as my dad's had been this morning. Was there a secret Wanted poster of *me* that only homeless people had seen?

"That's right, we all know who you are. Still, it's good you're trying to make amends," she said. She gave me a very faint wink. "And not a moment too soon, from the sound of things." And with that she hurried off down the street with Mason following close behind, her bag of cat food rattling loudly all the way.

Mapping Out a Turf War

AT EXACTLY THREE-THIRTY, WHEN THE WHOLE HOUSE WAS QUIET, I RAN downstairs with my skateboard and hurriedly put on my shoes.

I was trying to open the front door as silently as possible when Mum appeared in the hallway. "Where are you off to?" she asked. Lisa had the afternoon off, so Hercules was clinging on to Mum's back like a turtle shell. "You're still grounded, remember?"

"I forgot something at the soup kitchen," I said, which was kind of true—I had left the new T-shirt Mr. Cheng and Mei-Li had given me there. "Plus, I said I would help out at teatime."

Mum smiled. "Really?"

"Yeah."

"Mum, can I have soup in the kitchen too?" asked

Hercules, jumping off her back and squeezing past her to cling on to me instead. He had obviously been playing with some gold glitter because when I pushed him away, my trouser legs were covered in a trail of it.

"So . . . is it OK if I go?" I asked Mum.

"I guess. But take your jacket," she said as she suddenly reached out and ruffled my hair. "And come back straight after, all right? Hercules, how about we head to *our* kitchen for some cereal, and make that into our very own special kitchen soup?"

I stared at Mum's back as she headed down the corridor to the kitchen with Hercules bouncing behind her on his imaginary pogo stick. She hadn't ruffled my hair in years. Not since at least two Christmases ago. Putting my hair back the way it should be, I jumped onto my skateboard and headed out toward the high street.

I found the narrow alleyway between the pizza shop and the train station and ran through it and out on to the other side, heading to the back wall of the station, where the Catwoman lived.

Mei-Li was already there. She was sitting on the ground playing with two small cats. The Catwoman sat in her deckchair with a much larger gray cat purring on her lap. But Thomas wasn't with them.

A train thundered below my feet making the ground rattle as I went over to the Catwoman and Mei-Li. I stopped a few feet away.

"Don't be shy," said the Catwoman. "Take a seat and say hello to my babies."

Remembering how one of her babies had hissed at me last time, I went and sat down slowly on the floor next to Mei-Li. I waited for one of the cats to come up to me. But none of them did. Maybe they thought I was one of the boys who bullied the Catwoman too.

I watched as the cats walked around in circles like models on a catwalk. All of them had tiny brown collars with little tubes on them and bells that tinkled when they moved.

"They're just sniffing you out," whispered Mei-Li. "They did the same to me when I first came here with Dad."

I shrugged. I didn't want to touch the cats anyway in case they were dirty. What I really wanted was to know if Thomas was coming.

As if she could read my thoughts, the Catwoman picked up the cat on her lap like it was a baby, and held it out to me, saying, "He'll be here soon. Look."

I stared, not sure if I was meant to hold the cat like a baby too.

The Catwoman smiled, her half-yellow teeth poking out. "Take the note from Tabby's collar, boy," she said, giving Mei-Li a wink.

Sitting up on my knees, I looked more closely at Tabby's collar. Sticking out of the end of the little tube was a scrap of something white. Taking it, I unrolled a tiny crumpled sheet filled with curly handwriting, and read it aloud:

Will be with you by 4. Hope the boy isn't tricking us.
I'm close to breaking the code. Given Tabby some tuna.
Thomas

I frowned at the symbols and looked up at the Catwoman.

"What are these squiggles?" I asked.

"Latin alphabet symbols for 'L' and 'M,'" she explained, as if that made it any clearer. "All of us homeless folk have our own symbols—to make sure that whenever we need to send a message out, everyone knows for sure it's us. And LM is Thomas's."

I stared back at the tube on Tabby's collar, wondering why Thomas's symbol was "L" and "M." "So your cats . . . they take messages to people? Kind of like carrier pigeons?"

The Catwoman smiled. "Exactly. All I have to do is train them up and off they go."

"That's cool!" I exclaimed before I could stop myself.

"Yes, yes, it is rather," agreed the Catwoman.

"What's all this about, then?"

Mei-Li and the Catwoman and me all jumped at the deep voice booming from behind us.

"Thomas!" cried Mei-Li. She jumped up and gave him a hug. "You came!"

Feeling excited, I jumped up too. But then, feeling stupid, sat right back down.

"Of course I came! I'd do anything for the best baked potato maker in London," he said, winking at her. Then he turned and glared at me with such force that I could feel the heat coming out of his eyes. His beard had grown longer and his face looked darker than I remembered, and now that I could see him properly in the light and right in front of me, I knew for sure it had never been him at Piccadilly Circus. He was much shorter than the real thief had been, and his beard was less fluffy. He was still wearing his long black coat and yellow hat, but now he had a green scarf wrapped around his neck, as if it was December and not May.

"What have *you* got to say to me?" he said. "Other than 'sorry for trying to ruin your life,' that is?"

"I really am s-sorry," I stuttered, looking at the pavement so I could escape his eyes. I had never felt so bad about anything before. Not even when I had accidentally hurt Hercules or made Lavinia at school run away so fast that she had an asthma attack.

"For what?" said Thomas. "For pushing my trolley in the lake or for telling the police I'm the most wanted man in London?"

"Both," I said, scuffing my hand along the ground. "I really thought it was you. The real thief looked just like you."

Thomas didn't reply. Wanting to show him that I was serious about helping, I stood up and, taking the folded pieces of paper from my pocket, held them out to him.

"What are these?" asked Thomas, taking them.

I shrugged.

"Comic strips?" said Mei-Li, leaning over to look.

I shook my head. "Ideas. For how we could maybe catch the real thief and make sure the police stop arresting all the homeless people."

"Didn't have you down as an artist," said Thomas, turning over the second page.

"Is that you pointing out the actual thief?" Mei-Li grinned, pointing to a strip showing a whole line of men wearing false beards. I nodded.

"I personally quite like the idea of me in a cape," said Thomas, giving a sniff. "Decent ideas," he added as he handed me back my drawings without saying anything else. Mei-Li didn't say anything either, so I shoved them quickly back into my pocket, wishing I had never made them. Everyone clearly thought they were stupid.

There was a long silence, during which my legs itched to turn right around and leave. But I wasn't a coward, so I waited, holding my breath in the strange quiet.

"If you *really* want to help, you need to tell me everything you saw that night," said Thomas finally, cracking open the awkward silence that had fallen on us. "In as much detail as you can. Think you can do that?"

I let my breath go and nodded, and this time I looked up into his face. His two sharp eyes crashed right into mine, as if they were searching for something hidden away.

"Proceed," he ordered.

He sat down on the empty deck chair next to the Cat-woman and listened with his eyes shut tight and his fingers coming to a point on his lips as I described what I had seen at Piccadilly Circus for what felt like the hundredth time.

When I was finished, I waited for him to say something. But he continued sitting with his eyes shut for the longest time. Then without any warning, his eyes flew open and he leaned forward, making all of us—Mei-Li and the Catwoman too—jump.

"Now, I want you to describe him again. But this time, close your eyes. I want you to focus all your energies on just that man. Try and get your memory to scan over every single part of him—like an X-ray. Start off with his silver hair and describe him for me again, right down to the shoes he was wearing."

Scared by the look on Thomas's face, I shut my eyes and tried my best to remember that exact moment when the thief had bowed and looked up at the billboards. I described everything I could see in my mind, from the strange circle of silver hair on his head, to the remote control in his hand, to his wrinkly black coat, to the white sneakers that had seemed to glow in the dark, to the tiny shine of something gold on his finger. But there was nothing new to tell.

"Something shining on his finger?" asked Thomas. "You never mentioned that before."

"Didn't I?"

Mei-Li and the Catwoman shook their heads.

"Is it important?"

"Might be," said the Catwoman. "Was it a ring?"

I closed my eyes again and concentrated hard, making myself see the thief again as he took off his hat and held it out before him to take his bow.

"Yes," I said, scrunching my eyes shut even tighter.

"Can you see anything on it?" asked Thomas, his voice getting closer to my ears.

I shook my head. "Can't see—I'm too far away. But it was definitely gold—and round. And it was on the little finger of his right hand—he was holding out his hat with his right hand when he took the bow!"

"Ah, a pinkie ring," said Thomas as I opened my eyes. "At least that's a new clue we didn't have before!"

"What about the three lines on the fountain steps?" I asked. "Wasn't that a real clue? I tried looking it up online, but I couldn't find out what it meant."

"Oh, that's easy. Here, look." Thomas reached into his coat pocket, taking out a sheet of paper, which he unraveled to reveal a huge map of all the bus routes in London. It had been folded and unfolded so many times that it looked as if it was about to fall apart. On the front of it, written in big red letters, were the words "To our favorite Night Rider. From all the drivers at Transport for London."

I had never seen a map like it before, and I guess Mei-Li

hadn't either, because we both leaned in closer to see it in more detail. Each and every bus route had been given its own bright color, and they swirled and wound and spread past tiny drawings of parks and museums and palaces, like a giant octopus with its legs splitting out in all different directions. Across the map, Thomas had circled some of the places and written a number and a symbol beside them.

I followed Thomas's finger to a stop marked "Piccadilly Circus" and a drawing of a statue marked as "Eros"—which made me think of Mum and Dad and how they would have shaken their heads at the fact that even real maps had labeled it wrong. Underneath the picture, Thomas had drawn the symbol of the three diagonals I had seen being sprayed, and next to it, in the teeniest, tiniest capital letters, were the words "THIS IS NOT A SAFE PLACE."

"I've been recording the location, the object that was stolen, the symbol, and the meaning of that symbol for all the thefts," explained Thomas. "Take a look."

We crowded over the map, Mei-Li's fingers resting on the different colored bus routes, mine moving up to where a big "1" was circled. The 1 was next to the picture of a suitcase marked "PB." Without even knowing that I was doing it, I began to read all of Thomas's notes out loud.

"Number one. Location: Paddington Station. Stolen: Paddington Bear. Symbol: the spear. Meaning: Be ready to defend yourself.

Key Night Bus Routes: Central London

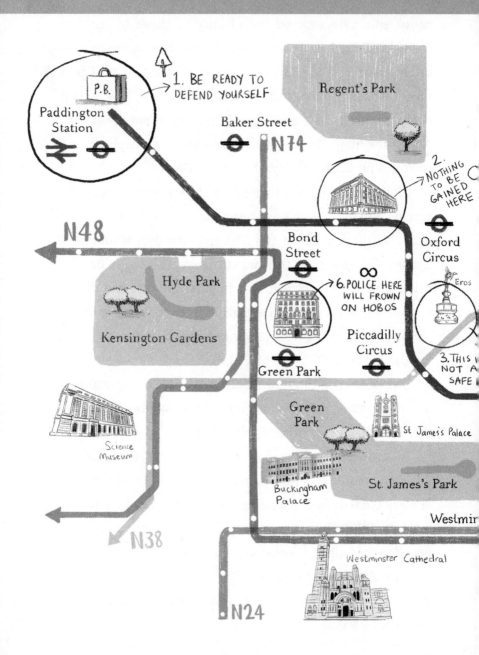

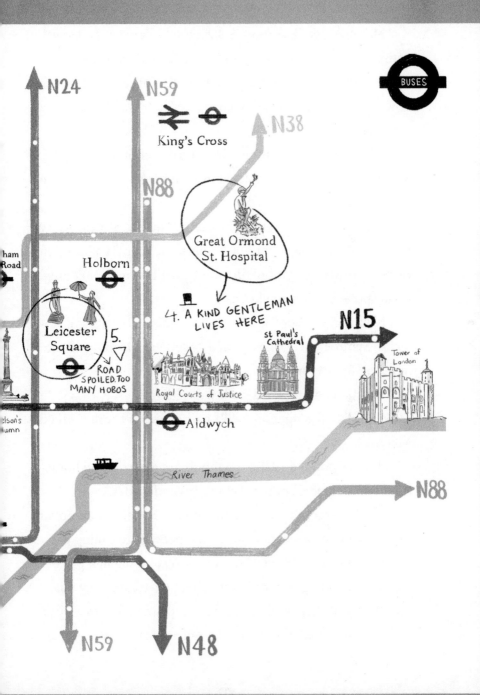

"Number two. Location: Selfridges. Stolen: winged angel. Symbol: a circle. Meaning: Nothing to be gained here.

"Number three. Location: Piccadilly Circus. Stolen: the bow of Eros. Symbol: three stripes. Meaning: This is not a safe place.

"Number four. Location: Great Ormond Street Hospital. Stolen: Tinker Bell. Symbol: hat. Meaning: A kind gentleman lives here.

"Number five. Location: Leicester Square. Stolen: Mary Poppins's umbrella, Charlie Chaplin's stick, and Paddington Bear's sandwich. Symbol: upside-down triangle. Meaning: Road spoiled, too many hobos.

"Number Six: Location: Fortnum and Mason. Stolen: lanterns. Symbol: two rings joined together. Meaning: Police here will frown on hobos."

I finished and took a deep breath. "Whoa."

"And all of the signs are really part of a secret code?" asked Mei-Li.

Thomas nodded. "All the symbols are a part of the homeless code. A global code, developed over decades."

"Or the 'tramp's code' or the 'hobo's code,'" interrupted the Catwoman. "Depending on what people are calling us."

"It's the one code we all use to warn someone if a place is dangerous, or to give them a hint about what help they might find there—if there's any to be had," explained Thomas. "We usually hide them pretty well so only someone who's truly one of us can find or understand them. This thief, whoever he is, must know someone from the streets—he's got to, to know the code exists and what the symbols mean. But he's definitely not *one* of us. No one who's had to sleep rough would ever give our code away. Especially not to the police or the press."

"I wish I knew what all the symbols meant and where to find them," said Mei-Li.

"Well, there's a fair few to learn," said the Catwoman, wrapping a cat's tail around her fingers. "Can take years to suss them all out. It's like an alphabet. Except you never get to see all the letters at once, and sometimes the meaning behind the letters change, or the letters get drawn different."

Now I knew why I hadn't been able to find anything on the internet—the code was still so secret that even the best search engines in the world hadn't found them out yet.

"You've forgotten to add the robbery from last night," said the Catwoman, giving Thomas a poke and leaning back in her deck chair.

"There was *another* one?" I asked. I really needed to start reading Dad's newspaper more.

Mei-Li nodded. "A dragon statue," she said. "It was on the news this morning."

"And not just any old dragon," added the Catwoman. "One that lived right outside the Royal Courts of Justice. Best place to get a divorce in all the land. Or so I've heard."

"I only got wind of it on the way here," said Thomas, drawing out a pen from his coat as if it were a sword. Bending over the map, he drew a circle around the picture of a building near the words "Fleet Street." Then he added a symbol of a long cross, and the words "Religious talk will get you a meal here" beside it.

"Now this is a strange one," he muttered.

"Why's it strange?" I asked.

"Because we have special codes to mark out courts or places where a judge might be found. But this sign is for a church or a member of the clergy," answered Thomas, stroking his beard the same way the Catwoman was stroking the cat on her lap. "See here." Thomas pointed to all the other robbery points. "Each symbol the thief's used so far is directly linked to the place he's robbed in some way. Even if it's in quite a funny way. For example." Thomas pointed to the picture of the spear next to Paddington Bear's suitcase. "This one is a warning—for everyone to 'defend' themselves. It might be a warning for us to defend ourselves against the thief and all the things he's about to do, but it's also funny—because why would anyone need to defend themselves against a cartoon bear who is himself in search of a home? Then this one— here," said Thomas, pointing to Selfridges and the circle next to it. "That sign is to signal that there's 'nothing to be gained here'—as in no food or water or help. But it's been drawn on a place which has everything you could ever need under one roof. Providing you have money, of course. So in actual fact, it really is of no value for someone who's homeless and looking for the basics of food and shelter. Then Fortnum and Mason—the two rings symbol there means police will frown on hobos. There might not be any real police there, but it's still a shop filled with posh people who really would 'frown' on us hobos—and call the police on us if they could. And the three lines at Piccadilly Circus there, warning us it's not a safe place, might be because it's a pickpocket hotspot."

"What about this one?" I asked, pointing at the hat drawn next to Great Ormond Street Hospital.

"That's a nicer one," said Thomas. "The kindly gentleman the symbol references could be J. M. Barrie—the man who wrote *Peter Pan* and gifted all the money from those books to help the sick people the hospital looks after. Or it could just be a nod to all the doctors inside. Or maybe it's Peter Pan himself. Who knows?"

"My *personal* favorite is Leicester Square," said the Catwoman, giving a chuckle as she pointed to it on the map. "Telling us there are 'too many hobos' in a place where Charlie Chaplin and Mary Poppins are sitting pretty, does have a whiff of the genius about it."

I frowned at Mei-Li, who gave me a frown right back. I was glad she wasn't so much of a teacher's pet that she could understand why both the Catwoman and Thomas were now chuckling.

"Aaaah," said Thomas, seeing our blank faces. "Because they're both without homes, see?" he explained. "Charlie Chaplin, the world's most famous hobo. A tramp even by name."

"And Mary Poppins?" asked Mei-Li.

"Oh, she's always flitting from one place to the next," said the Catwoman. "Granted she's a governess and she gets paid, but she doesn't really have a home either."

"Oh, yeeeeeeah," said Mei-Li and me together.

"So you see, all the symbols have some sort of link to the place they've been sprayed on—even if it's a sort of humorous, sarcastic one. But yesterday's theft of the dragon isn't linked to the symbol of the cross that's been drawn. Not as far as I can figure out. So why is that? Has he used the wrong sign? Or is he teasing us?" He sighed. "Just as I'm figuring it all out, he throws me a curveball. There just isn't any pattern that's obvious with this thief. Except one, which is—"

"None of the robberies are outside zone one," interrupted Mei-Li.

"Clever kid," remarked the Catwoman as Mei-Li gave her ponytail an extra-high flick. "She can see a turf war when it's staring her in the face, even if no one else can."

"You mean a turf war like gangs in movies have?" gasped Mei-Li.

"Not quite," laughed Thomas. "Look here. What does all this bit of London have in common?" He waved his hand over the whole of zone one.

"It has all the most expensive shops?" said Mei-Li.

Thomas shook his head. "What else does it have? More than anywhere else in London?"

"Parks? Palaces? Animals?" tried Mei-Li again.

The Catwoman shook her head. "I'll give you a clue," she said, and pointed to herself and Thomas.

"Homeless people," I cried.

"Exactly!" said Thomas. "There's thousands of us sleeping rough in this area of London alone. And lots of people don't like it. It's a turf war that's been going on for as long as the city has been here. Businesses and governments want to kick us out."

"Instead of trying to help us," added the Catwoman, shaking her head.

"So you think the thief is stealing all these strange things . . . and drawing those signs . . . so he can make the police think that . . ." Mei-Li didn't finish her sentence. Instead, she covered her mouth with her hands.

"She's got it," whispered the Catwoman. She looked over at me to see if I had got it too.

I had, but I was too busy thinking about what Thomas had said about it being a "turf war" to say anything. The whole thing was starting to sound like my computer game!

On level nine, a group of aliens called the Zuldacs were racing me to take over a land called Exted. Instead of using my small army against the massive Zuldac one, I secretly put up flags everywhere, to make it seem as if the Zuldacs were *already* claiming Exted as their own. That made the Exted people rise up and begin to fight the Zuldacs back. And while they were busy fighting each other, I swept in for the real invasion and won.

It was the same in *this* case too! The thief was blaming the people he was trying to get rid of for crimes they hadn't committed and, by making everyone else hate them too, was reaching his goal! The only difference was that the Invisible Thief was using yellow signs instead of flags to start the fights. The only thing we had to figure out was what he was trying to distract everyone from.

Flags. White flags . . . with writing on them . . . and two blue dragons . . . flags that had made Hercules giggle about toy-lets! And like a thunder crack, it came to me.

"Hector? You all right?" asked Thomas, placing a hand on my shoulder. "You've gone all pale, lad."

"The toilet signs," I whispered, tapping the map. "The toilet signs are the real flags!"

The Pass to Freedom

"TOILETS?"

Mei-Li, Catwoman, Thomas, and the cats were all staring up at me, puzzled.

"My brother, Hercules, saw them," I explained. "'To Let' signs shaped like flags on all the buildings next to where the thefts took place. The same exact signs—white ones with two blue dragons. There was one on the platform where Paddington Bear was stolen, hanging above an old café. And lots on the flats next to the children's hospital, *and* on the office buildings near Piccadilly Circus. What if *that* is the real sign of the invasion and everything else is fake?"

"It makes sense," said Catwoman, tapping zone one on the map with her finger. "This is prime real estate. *The* most expensive part of one of *the* most expensive cities in the world. The last thing any property developer trying to rent out a building wants is a bunch of homeless people driving prices down."

"So stage some robberies of public property, get us blamed, and drive us out," said Thomas, nodding. "Easy! And you're right, those signs—the ones with the blue dragons—they are everywhere. I see them all the time on my night rides . . . maybe they really could be the missing link!"

"Not just a head of hair, are you, Hector?" Catwoman smiled.

I shrugged and gave a small smile back, pushing my hair away from my face.

"WHAT about the 'To Let' signs?" asked Mei-Li, looking more confused than I had ever seen her. "I don't get it!"

Wondering how a teacher's pet could possibly not get it, I explained everything in more detail. Her eyes slowly widened like two balloons being blown up as she finally understood.

"But why would an invading force blame homeless people?" she asked as soon as I had finished.

"Why not?" asked Thomas. "We can't defend ourselves, and there's no one to fight for us. We're just problems, remember? Drunkards and drug addicts and beggars who people are already frightened of. Sitting targets."

Mei-Li shook her head. "That's horrible."

"The thief's got to be somebody with a lot of money and power to make all of this happen," muttered Catwoman. "And connections too. A property owner with buildings all over London would have loads of places to hide the statues. How are we ever going to catch them?"

"Hold on." Flipping his map over, Thomas's finger ran down a small list of dates. "See here," he said. "I've been making a list of when the thief's been striking. Most of the time there isn't a pattern. Sometimes they'll strike two nights in a row, and other times it will be a week between thefts. But there *is* one thing I've spotted."

His finger jumped from one date on the list down to another, and then a third. "They've struck every Saturday since the thefts began . . . all at different times of the night."

"But *today's* Saturday," I said slowly.

"And we haven't got a clue about where he might strike next—or what time," added Mei-Li.

We all fell silent. Then, suddenly, Catwoman pushed the cat that had been sleepily purring on her lap on to the floor. "Thomas," she exclaimed. "The cross . . . why did he use the sign of the cross by the stolen dragon at the courts?"

Thomas shrugged. "Maybe he's getting bored and scribbling any old sign now? Maybe it doesn't matter to him."

"*Or*," said Catwoman, her brown-green eyes shining. "What if he's made a mistake? What if that sign was meant to be left at the *next* target?"

"What does the cross sign mean again?" I asked.

"It's one we'd leave at a church, or at a place that has something to do with a church," she explained. "Like the home of a priest."

"Maybe you're right," said Thomas. "Maybe tonight's target

is a church." He sighed. "But there are hundreds of churches across London and plenty of them have statues."

We all crowded around the map and stared at it as if it might give us the answer.

"Are the robberies all going from this side of London to this one?" asked Mei-Li, tilting her head and sliding her hand down from Paddington Station to the Royal Courts of Justice. "Or are they all mixed up and jumping backward and forward?"

Thomas flipped his map over and then back again and counted things on his fingers.

"They've been jumping back and forth," he said finally. "But only very slightly. The majority of the robberies *have* been moving down from west to east."

"Good spot, darling," said Catwoman, giving Mei-Li's arms a squeeze.

I gave her a thumbs-up too.

"And look," added Thomas. "Most of them have been along one main route! The longest night bus route there is . . ."

"And the most expensive too!" said Catwoman. "It hits all the hot spots of London."

We followed his finger as he traced a bright pink line labeled "N15" that started at Paddington Station, then ran down to Selfridges, passed by the statue of Anteros, went across Leicester Square, and carried on past the Royal Courts of Justice.

The only two places that had been left out were the thefts at Fortnum and Mason and Great Ormond Street Hospital, which were on the opposite sides of the city to each other.

Thomas's finger slowed to a halt as it reached the picture of a church labeled "St. Paul's Cathedral."

"No," gasped Catwoman.

"Might just be," said Thomas. "It's the next major stop on the bus route."

"I doubt they'll be hopping on a night bus to get to their robberies," said Catwoman, shaking her head. "Besides, they can't hit St. Paul's tonight. It's VE Day tomorrow, remember? They'll be having a choir concert tonight and a light show too. It'll be packed solid until at least gone midnight—and even after that the whole place will still be lit up. It would be madness. . . ."

"But that gives us a time—a window of when they might act," said Thomas.

"And don't forget the thief has that special remote control," I reminded everyone. "I saw them. They turned every single light off with one click."

"And imagine it," said Thomas, jumping up from his chair and starting to pace up and down excitedly. "Imagine robbing St. Paul's the night before VE Day! It would be a coup! Robbing one of the richest cathedrals with some of the most expensive statues in the world, on one of the most important days in the world. It sounds like exactly what this thief would do! And the public would be furious. If people weren't already scared and angry and ready to drive us all out before, they definitely would be after that!"

"*If* we're right, that is," interrupted Mei-Li.

"Let's tell the police," I said, hoping we had figured it all out. If we had, we would probably be heroes by tomorrow morning! I would have to share being famous with Mei-Li now since she knew everything too, but I didn't mind, so long as everyone knew it was mainly me who had helped catch the thief. Now all the police had to do was go and watch the church and catch the real thief.

Catwoman laughed. "Tell the police? They'd never believe the likes of us," she said, gesturing to herself and Thomas.

"Or us," added Mei-Li, looking at me. "We're just kids. They'd think we were making things up. Plus, they definitely wouldn't believe *you*. You've only just told them Thomas was the thief."

Thomas suddenly stopped walking and clicked his fingers with a loud snap.

"I've got a plan," he cried. "Providing we're right about this, of course. But I can't do it by myself. I'm going to need some help . . . from someone brave enough and small enough to get in through a very tiny window."

Turning to me and Mei-Li, he swooped down on us like a human eagle and caught us each by the hand.

"Which one of you can come with me?" he asked, his eyebrows squeezed together tight. "And help me catch a thief?"

"This is stupid," I muttered as me and Mei-Li hurried back down the alleyway and out on to the high street. "It'll never work. He's mad."

"He's not mad," said Mei-Li. "He's brave. And the plan is brave. You just have to be brave too and not mess it up."

I glared at Mei-Li. It should have been her going tonight, not me. Who had to share a bedroom with their grandparents anyway? How was that even allowed? Or maybe it was a lie so that she could get out of helping!

"I'll come to yours before dinner," said Mei-Li. "To give you my grandad's bus pass."

"DON'T ring the doorbell or anything," I ordered. "My bedroom window is at the front of the house, on the right. Just throw something at it, and I'll open it up so you can toss it in."

"Why can't I just knock for you like a normal person?" asked Mei-Li. "I can say you left something at the soup kitchen."

"No!" I said, more loudly than I should have. "I really don't want anyone . . ." I stopped myself, but it was too late.

Mei-Li stopped walking. "You don't want anyone to see me? Is that what you were going to say?"

I wanted to tell her no, but I knew she'd know it was a lie. Because the truth was, I didn't want anyone to see her at my house. Especially not Helen, whose friends all had brothers and sisters who went to my school. If Katie and Will heard about it, they would never shut up.

Mei-Li's whole face turned red. "FORGET IT," she shouted. Then, without another word, she turned back around and began walking off as fast as she could. I looked at her, wondering if she was still going to get me the bus pass I needed and wishing I had kept my mouth shut tight.

The Night Riders

WHEN I GOT HOME, I WAS FEELING SO TWITCHY THAT I LOCKED MYSELF away in my room until tea. As soon as that was over, I ran back upstairs and looked out of my window every few minutes to see if Mei-Li was coming. But she wasn't there at six o'clock, or at six-thirty, or at six-forty-five. By the time the clock on my computer said seven, I was sure she wasn't coming. Which meant I wouldn't be able to help Thomas catch the thief. Which meant nobody would know that I hadn't got Thomas in trouble on purpose. If, of course, the thief was even going to be at St. Paul's Cathedral and not somewhere else tonight.

I sat down on my bed and thought about what to do. If only I had kept my mouth shut and not let Mei-Li know that I didn't want anyone to see me with her. But why did she care so much anyway? Why did *I* care so much?

Tap!

A stone hit my window and rattled down the slates on the roof over the front door.

I jumped to my feet.

TAP!

Another bigger stone came hurtling to the glass.

I ran over and threw open the large side window.

Mei-Li was outside the front gate, crouching behind the small garden wall.

I waved and smiled.

But she didn't smile back.

Taking something bright blue out of her coat pocket, she stood up and, looking around quickly to make sure no one was coming, threw it as hard as she could at my window.

THUMP.

It hit the windowsill and fell straight down into the yard.

Covering her mouth with her hands to stop herself from squealing, Mei-Li crouched back down. Before I could tell her that I would run down and get it, she squeaked open the front gate, grabbed the bright blue object, then ran out.

I leaned out of my window as far as I could without falling and waited. Mei-Li drew back her arm again. This time, the small flat parcel twirled through the air like a ninja dart and smacked me right in the face.

"Ooooooowwwwwwwww!" I groaned, waving to show Mei-Li that I had caught it. But she was already gone. She hadn't even stopped to wish me good luck.

Rubbing my face, I closed the window and opened up the blue wallet. Inside it, on the left side, was Mei-Li's grandad's senior bus pass, with a photo and a name and date stamped on it. I stared at the photo, wondering how Mei-Li thought I could ever get away with pretending to be her eighty-seven-year-old grandad. For one thing, his face looked like melting wax, and his eyes were so droopy and long they looked as if they were trying to reach the floor. For another, he had shocking white hair all over his head. I was definitely going to need a hat and a really long scarf and my puffer jacket.

Opposite the bus pass was a torn bit of paper tucked away inside the plastic. It said, "Don't lose this. Good luck. Mei-Li."

Snapping the wallet shut and putting it into my pocket, I snuck my winter puffer coat from the hallway and borrowed Dad's posh walking cap and his extra-long striped scarf from the hook on his bedroom door and stuffed them all into my rucksack, along with some chocolate bars in case I got hungry. When there was nothing left to do, I played my games until it was time for lights-out. Mum and Dad always said good night at nine-thirty and wanted our lights off by ten when they were home, so I knew they would check for any lights under my door after then.

Lying down in the dark, I waited for the luminous hands of the clock to tell me it was eleven o'clock. The minute hand crawled its way along the clock face, slower than I had ever seen it move before.

Ten-eleven . . .

Ten-fifteen . . .

Ten-twenty-one . . .

Ten-twenty-three . . .

Ten-thirty . . .

I could feel myself dozing off. I slapped my cheeks and pulled my eyes open with my fingers. There was no way I could fall asleep—not tonight!

Ten-thirty-three . . .

Ten-forty . . .

At ten-forty-two, I could still hear Mum and Dad downstairs, laughing at something on the TV.

By ten-forty-five, I couldn't wait anymore and slowly crept out of bed. Trying not to make the floorboards creak, I piled a heap of clothes under my covers and shaped it to look like a long body, just like I had seen in movies. Then I pulled my overstuffed rucksack on to my back and headed to the window. It was my only way out. The front door was too close to where Mum and Dad were, and chances were they had already turned on the alarm for it anyway.

The street outside looked quiet and empty, as if it was drowsy and half-asleep too. I listened and waited. Mum and Dad laughed loudly again. Taking my chance, I quickly undid the latch and pushed open the big window. It gave off a loud squeak, making me instantly pause and listen. There was no movement on the stairs, so after waiting another moment, I climbed onto the ledge, swinging one leg out and over into the air.

Sitting in the middle of the windowsill, I looked down. All I had to do was drop onto the little roof running below me and then lower myself to the gravel below. Without making a single noise. It had looked easy in the daylight, but now the ground seemed so far away it might as well have been seventeen floors down.

I thought of what Mei-Li had said. *You just have to be brave too and not mess it up.*

I'd show her!

I gripped the side of the ledge and wriggled myself out and over and down. Clinging on to the last bit of my window with my fingers, I felt around with my toes for the roof below. But it was too far away—and my legs were too short. I couldn't reach it. With a breath, I let go, hoping the roof was only a short drop away.

THUD!

THUMP!

CRASH!

MEOOOOOOOOOOOW!

CRUNCH!

I opened my eyes. I was lying on my back on top of my rucksack in the garden. I had made it all in one go!

A light clicked on from behind the front door.

I rolled myself at top speed into a shrub and lay flat on my tummy, trying not to get any dirt into my mouth.

The garden lit up as the front door swung open.

"What is it?" called Mum from inside the house.

At that moment, the cat I had disturbed meowed again from somewhere nearby.

"Just next door's cat," Dad shouted back. I heard the door shut as he went back inside.

Feeling more grateful than I had ever felt for the existence of cats, I waited for a few more seconds, before rolling out of the shrub like a spy, and making my way to the front gate. Wishing I could have brought my skateboard with me, I began to run as fast as I could to the main road and past the railings of the empty park. It was all locked up and shining in the moonlight like a playing field built for ghosts. Halfway down the road, I could see the light of a bus stop, and the shape of an old man sitting underneath it.

"There you are," said Thomas, getting up from the bright red plastic bench he had been sitting on. Looking at me, his beard made way for a grin. "What happened to you? Trouble leaving paradise?"

I looked down and realized I had two squashed slugs and a trail of dirt running all the way down the front of my hoodie.

"EUGH!" I cried, jumping back and trying to get away from myself.

"Hold still," said Thomas, chuckling as he swiped the slugs away from me and sent them flying into the night air like half-melted gummy bears. "Now hurry—the bus will be here in a few minutes. Malcolm is never late."

Nodding, I quickly pulled out my puffer coat and Dad's

scarf and hat from my rucksack and put them on. Thomas grabbed the scarf and twirled me around like a giant piece of cotton candy until everything on my face except my eyes were covered.

"Hmmmm," said Thomas, stepping back to look at me. "You're not tall enough to pass for a grown man. Hunch your back right down—as if you're looking for a penny on the ground."

I did what he said.

"Good, good. Keep that scarf high around your face, and your hat pulled low so none of your hair shows—and that back bent right over—and shake a bit when you walk too. Think it might be the only way we can pass you off for an eighty-seven-year-old night rider. If no one looks too closely, of course." He frowned. "We'll have to do something about your hair."

He tried to push my floppy brown hair back underneath Dad's hat. But my hair was too slippery and long, and the hat was too small.

"Sorry, lad, we'll have to do a hat swap," said Thomas, taking off Dad's cap and plonking his yellow hat on my head instead. I promised my head I would clean it with disinfectant and the strongest shampoo ever invented as soon as this was all over.

"Right, now remember," said Thomas as he helped me zip up my rucksack and put it back on over my bulky layers.

"We've got two buses to catch to get to St. Paul's. When we're getting on, act sleepy, look at the floor and just grunt when you show the pass. Got that? And whatever you do, do NOT make eye contact."

As he talked, a big red bus appeared from around the corner, getting closer and closer until it eventually came to a halt in front of us.

"Here we go," Thomas whispered. "Ready?"

Before I could respond, the doors whacked open and a voice called out, "Hey, Thomas, all right?"

"Hey, Malcolm! Yeah, just the usual chills," said Thomas, rubbing his arms as he climbed on board. "Got a friend coming with me tonight. Come on, Mr. Zhou, up you get, old-timer!"

Coughing to pretend I was old and bending over to look for that invisible penny, I climbed up on to the step of the bus. Getting out the Freedom Pass, I held it out, my eyes looking at nothing but the shiny gray plastic floor.

"No need for that, Mr. Zhou," said Malcom. "Any night rider who's a friend of Thomas's is welcome aboard my boat!" And with a loud *ding-ding,* he slammed the doors shut and launched his bus-boat deep into the pitch-black sea of the roads ahead.

Paul and the Midnight Mass

SITTING ON THE TOP DECK, I WATCHED AS THE HEADLIGHTS SHONE OUT like extra-large flashlights onto a road that was as black as the night sky.

I couldn't believe I had done it! I had actually run away from home without getting caught and was now on a bus pretending to be an eighty-seven-year-old Asian man, to go and catch a thief with a man whose trolley I had drowned in a lake. It was like a strange dream.

I could feel Thomas staring at me from his bus seat across the aisle. I glanced at him. He wasn't blinking and was stroking his beard.

By the time the bus had reached the next stop, I couldn't take it anymore and asked, "What?"

"Ah," he said, stroking his beard even slower. "Don't mind me. I tend to stare when I'm thinking. And right now, I'm thinking some mighty interesting thoughts. About your being so eager to help me catch this thief. Despite appearances and all the things you've done, it seems like you're not all bad."

I went back to looking out of the windows but felt my ears heating up under the layers of scarf.

"I was also thinking about Mei-Li," continued Thomas. "And the soup kitchen. Catwoman told me you've been helping out there. But something tells me that you might not be going back after all this is over. Maybe once you get a pat on the back and some of that reward money too, you won't be thinking about helping Mei-Li out again?"

A burst of volcanic flame shot up through my chest. Pulling the boiling hot scarf away from my face, I shouted, "You're wrong! And I don't even know about any stupid reward money!"

"Really?" asked Thomas. "You quite sure about that, son?"

"DON'T call me 'son'! I'm NOT your son," I yelled, before I could stop myself. As soon as the words left my mouth, I wished I could have caught them with a net and stuffed them all back in again.

Thomas became still for a few seconds and then looked away, nodding at his reflection in the window.

"I—I didn't mean . . . ," I stuttered, hating the way his silence was making me feel.

Thomas put his hands up and looked at me with a smile that wasn't real, saying, "Forget it. Didn't mean to get so personal. It won't happen again."

I stared at my hands as they gripped the railing in front of me. The bus had come to a second stop. We still had six more to go. I wished it was all over already.

A woman and a small boy wearing summer jackets but looking cold thanks to the sudden coolness of the night came up the stairs and went to sit right at the back. Thomas glanced at them and then turned back to me. "Look, Hector. It's OK. I'm not really interested in your reasons for helping me do this. All I care about is that you don't hurt our Mei-Li. She's been through enough as it is."

"What do you mean?" I asked, forgetting I was angry and looking over at Thomas. "What do you mean, she's been through enough as it is?"

Thomas narrowed his eyes at me. "Has Mei-Li ever mentioned her mum to you? Or have you ever asked yourself why she works so hard in the kitchen and in school when she should be out being a kid? Or why she's never brought a friend to the kitchens before you?"

I shook my head, not wanting to tell Thomas that I had never once thought about any of those things because Mei-Li was a teacher's pet, and I hadn't ever cared about anyone who was one of those before. Not enough to be their friend anyway.

"Scooch up," ordered Thomas as a large group of noisy men and women dressed in sequins and leather jackets all ran up the stairs singing and shouting at each other.

"A night rider's nightmare," he whispered as he came and sat next to me.

The bus launched off again, and I waited for Thomas to explain.

"You ever heard of leukemia, Hector?"

I gave a single nod. "It's a disease, isn't it?"

"Yes," Thomas said with a sigh. "Mei-Li's mum had it. Some people get better and some people don't. Mei-Li's mum didn't, and she died last year."

"Oh," I said, my nose beginning to tickle. I rubbed it hard and looked down at Thomas's old hands.

"A few months after she died," he continued, "her dad decided they should move. He couldn't bear to live in their house without her. So he made Mei-Li and her grandparents move here. For Mei-Li, that meant leaving all her friends behind. She and her dad volunteer at the kitchen because her mum worked for a similar charity back where they used to live. A charity that helped homeless women get off the streets. Women who just needed a bit of extra help."

"You mean like Catwoman?"

"Among many others."

"But how's she being helped if she's still *on* the streets?" I asked. "Especially when she's so—" I stopped myself, remembering that Thomas was old too.

"It's OK. You can say it: 'old.'" Thomas smiled.

I nodded as the bus sped past a bus stop and gathered speed.

"For some people—like Catwoman—even though she's a grandmother and has—"

"Hold on, Catwoman has *grandkids*?" I asked, feeling shocked. I had never thought about anyone who was homeless having children or grandchildren.

"Four of them," said Thomas, smiling. "They're beautiful. She's got photos of them inside her tent."

"But how come she's not living with them?" I asked as the bus juddered to a halt. We only had one more stop now. "Why does she stay in her tent?"

"Sometimes, after a long time living a certain way, it's easier to stick with what you know," said Thomas. "Back when she was young, Catwoman got bullied into doing some bad things and, well, she started believing she was a bad person. She couldn't really go back to being herself again. People like Mei-Li's mum and everyone at the kitchen, they help hurt folks like Catwoman get back to being themselves. Slowly, they help them start to remember good things, and help them believe that they *deserve* good things too. But that can take years. And sometimes it's easier to stay with your cats and the friends you've got. See, we might not have much, but we've got each other. And if you have to say goodbye to that, then we really *don't* have a home. Ah! We're here," he said, pressing the bell.

The bus voice announced, "Next stop: Aldwych." As the bus slowed down, I thought about Catwoman and all the people at the soup kitchen who needed to be taught how to remember who they were again because they had been bullied. And how they had been made to forget all the good things about themselves.

And how I didn't want to be someone who made people forget who they were . . .

"Scarf up, and off we get lad!" whispered Thomas. "Quickly now!"

Clambering down the stairs and waving goodbye to the driver, Thomas led me back out into the street. The air felt even cooler after the warmth of the bus, and I wrapped my dad's scarf around my face even tighter.

"Shouldn't be too long," said Thomas, leaning against the bus stop. Behind us, a woman with giant headphones on was half standing and half dancing as she waited for her bus. Spotting Thomas and me, she took a step away and turned her back to us. With the mud stains on my knees and my weird scarf and woolen hat, I remembered that I looked homeless now too.

Starting to shiver, I moved my arms and legs and feet to try and make myself warmer. Just as I was wondering if we were even going to make it to the cathedral before dawn, a bus rolled up beside us, a big "N15" glowing out at us from the front.

The woman muttered, "Finally," and pushed past me and Thomas onto the bus. It made me want to stick out my leg and trip her for being so rude to Thomas, but he held me back and let her pass.

"Remember, eyes down, pass up, and keep close behind me," whispered Thomas, before stepping onto the bus and showing his pass.

I held mine up too, but the woman behind the wheel didn't seem to care and was driving away again before I had even got on properly.

"We'll stay down here," said Thomas, grabbing a seat next to the door. "It's just three stops now."

I silently sat down next to him. Right at the back of the bus in the corner, I could see someone half lying down on the seat, a coat covering up the top part of their body. London, it seemed, was full of night riders.

"Next stop: Chancery Lane . . ."

"Next stop: Shoe Lane . . ."

At each stop, the doors opened to let people off and let gusts of air blow in. I was feeling hot now that we were back on a warm bus wearing so many layers and was glad we were sitting by the doors. Thomas had his eyes closed, and I wondered if he was thinking the same thoughts as me. Thoughts like: What were we going to do if we were wrong and the Invisible Thief never showed up? Or what if they had been and gone and we had missed them completely?

"Next stop: Ludgate Circus."

"That's us," whispered Thomas.

As the doors glided open, I shuffled out after him and onto the empty street. Looming before us like a giant stone ship was St. Paul's Cathedral. Except instead of being white and still, its whole face had been turned into one big cinema screen. Constantly changing pictures of men and women in army uniforms flashed up on to its pillars and bricks and across its golden clock that told us it was nearly eleven-forty-five. It was the VE Day celebrations just like Catwoman had described.

Grabbing my arm, Thomas pulled me behind the corner of a shop and whispered, "Let's keep a lookout here for now. The concert has ended, so the cathedral should be empty. Keep your eye out for any strange movement. Remember, we don't know if they might try to take something from Queen Victoria over there, or target something inside. If we're at the right church, that is . . ."

I peeked around at the giant milky-white statue of a woman with a golden crown on her head. She was carrying a stick and ball as if she was off to play a game. Maybe this really was the place the thief would try and steal from next. He would find it super easy to hang down from the queen's neck to take all her sports equipment.

As we waited, I looked around to see if there were any lumps pretending to sleep in doorways that might suddenly start moving and wriggling like a human plant. But there weren't. There was only a couple holding hands and walking toward the cathedral on the other side of the street, kissing and giggling loudly.

"Thomas, I think we're at the wrong place," I whispered, tugging on his arm. "The traffic lights and building lights and everything are all working. Nothing's been switched off."

But Thomas was looking up at the cathedral and grinning. "I think we're at *exactly* the right place. Look. Up there. The light *inside* the cathedral isn't on."

"What light?"

Thomas pointed up to the second row of pillars that stood above the cathedral's giant doors. "See the window there?" he asked. "Well, it's *always* lit. In all my twenty years on the streets and on the buses, I've never seen it go a single night without being lit."

"Maybe they've switched it off tonight because of the VE show?" I suggested.

Thomas shook his head. "That light wouldn't be switched off today of all days. It's meant to be a sign of perpetual hope to everyone who sees it. I think your thief is inside already, picking out something priceless to steal."

"Even more priceless than the queen's golden stick?" I asked, wondering what could be more expensive than an actual stick made of gold.

"Infinitely," whispered Thomas. "We need to hurry. Come on, there's no one around now."

Moving quickly, Thomas led me past a row of shuttered shops and up to an office building standing directly opposite the side wall of the cathedral and surrounded by a row of short black gates. Behind the gates, at the top of the stairs, next to a shiny black office door, was a golden sign with two swords crossed like an "X" and the words "Administration Offices of St. Paul's Cathedral" stamped across it.

Glancing around to check we were still alone, Thomas opened the swinging gate. But instead of climbing up the steps that led to the office door, he turned to go down some steeper steps that looked as if they led to an underground cave. I followed him down, and we reached a smaller door with a small round window above it, and a much bigger window next to it.

Thomas looked down at me. "Think you can do it? It's the only way to get in without being seen or setting any alarms off."

I wanted to shake my head. It was a crazy idea! How was I supposed to fit in through that tiny round window? I was way too big. And that window was too small—and high—and probably not even open! But I thought of Mei-Li's warning that the plan was brave and would work only if I was too, so I gave a silent nod instead.

"Shhh! Wait!" said Thomas, freezing.

I froze too. On the pavement above us, we heard footsteps ringing out. They crossed over us and faded into the distance.

"OK," nodded Thomas, helping me take off my rucksack, my puffer coat, and my dad's scarf.

"Keep the hat on—just in case," whispered Thomas, giving

it a pat. "Now remember, there's no alarm on the window because it's so small. Just push through gently, make sure you land safely, and then come unlock the big window for me. Remember, you have to press the green button on the wall— if you don't, the alarm will go off when you try and get the latch open."

"'K," I whispered, too scared to say anything else.

"Brave lad," Thomas whispered back, handing me a small torch. Hoisting me up onto his shoulders, he balanced himself and me as I reached up and touched the round window. Just like he had promised, it swung inward at the touch of my fingertips. I tried to pull myself up to the opening, but my body was too heavy.

"*Higher,*" I whispered. Thomas groaned as he pushed me up just high enough for me to hook both my arms inside the opening. Pulling my body through until only my legs were sticking outside, I hesitated; then, with a deep breath, I tipped myself forward and landed with a thump and half a head roll on to the carpet below. It was a good thing Thomas had made me keep his hat on!

Switching on the torch, I found the room on my right that led to the front windows, just like Thomas had described.

Reaching the huge white curtains shielding the windows, I pulled them aside and saw Thomas waiting outside, stroking his beard so hard that it looked as if he might pull it right off. On seeing me he gave me a thumbs-up. I found the green button on the wall, pressed it, and, grabbing the latch, slid the bottom half of the window up and open. Dumping his own coat and hat and my rucksack outside, Thomas knelt down and squeezed into the room like a shadow.

"Brilliant work, Hector. But you're never to do this again," he said, patting my arm. "This is the last time you break into a historic building."

I grinned, wondering how many detentions Mr. Lancaster would give me if he could see me now.

"Now, are you sure you don't want to wait here?" whispered Thomas.

"No! You promised I could help catch him!"

"Sure?"

I nodded like I had never nodded in my life before.

"All right, then. Stick close."

Leading me out into the corridor, Thomas stopped at a small wooden door under the stairs. He swung it open to reveal an empty space.

"Hold the flashlight steady," he whispered as he knelt down beside a large metal trapdoor that was built into the floor inside the space. Just like he had told us it would be.

"Remember. Don't breathe in too deep. Short breaths until we get to the end, OK? It's important to keep your breaths short and consistent to save air. It's not a long way to the cathedral, but it's underground and it's deep and slippery—and that can make it *feel* long. At least, that's how I remember it from the days I used to work for the archives team."

I was too excited to reply, and Thomas was too excited to wait for an answer. I held the flashlight as still as I could as he grabbed the metal ring and slowly lifted the trapdoor open. Beneath it was a short flight of stairs that led down into a pool of dark nothingness.

"Here we come, Paul," promised Thomas as he climbed down into the hole and was quickly swallowed up by the tunnel below. As I followed him down, the walls and floors all around us began to tremble. Paul's clock was striking midnight, and his chimes were ringing out to tell the world that a new day was about to begin.

$$\frac{2}{10}$$

The Man with Five Faces

TRYING MY BEST NOT TO COUGH IN THE HEAVY, DUSTY AIR, I SCUTTLED after Thomas, following the flashlight's circle of light to the end of the tunnel.

"Shhhh!" whispered Thomas as we finally reached a short iron ladder that led up to a small wooden hatch. "Don't move until I say so."

Climbing halfway up the ladder, he switched off the flashlight. I reached out and touched the walls of the tunnel. There wasn't a single bit of light from anywhere, and nothing to help me see—just like that night in Piccadilly Circus.

From above my head, I heard a quiet creak that echoed all around us.

Then silence.

"Thomas?"

Another "Shhhh!" ricocheted off the walls.

I waited, not knowing if the extra-loud thumping noise was coming from somewhere in the cathedral or from my chest.

"Give me your hands," ordered Thomas's voice above me.

I reached up toward the sound of it and banged my hand against the ladder instead. A loud metal ringing sound ran down the tunnel and back up again.

"Sorry," I whispered, trying again more slowly. This time, my fingers found the tips of Thomas's and grabbed on. Clutching my wrists and then my sides, he pulled me up like a bucket from a well and set me down on a cold, hard piece of marble. From the ceiling above us, I could hear the sound of buzzing, as if a giant fly was trapped in between the floors.

Switching on the torch, Thomas flooded the room with white light. We were in a big underground hall, with huge statues and archways all squashed down by a low ceiling. On one side of the room was a long glass room that said: "Gift Shop," and on the opposite wall were signs for the bathrooms. Up ahead was a café with all the tables and chairs left out and positioned in between gigantic stone statues.

But out of everything I could see, it was the floor that was most interesting. It was covered in fancy, swirly writing and patterned with long rectangular slabs. After a few seconds, I realized the writing spelled out the names of people and told stories of who they had been before they died. When Thomas had said the only way to get into the cathedral without breaking anything or setting the alarms off was through a tunnel that led into the church basement, I hadn't thought it was going to be basement with lots of people buried underneath it.

"We're in the crypt," explained Thomas. "Look there." He pointed the flashlight up ahead to where a kitchen stood in the shadows behind a long counter. "Notice how none of the machines are on? Not even the fridge lights. Somehow they've cut the building off without cutting off the whole grid. Which means none of the alarms will be working. Clever. Come on. This way."

He ran to a set of heavy glass doors, pulled one open, and motioned for me to hurry. We reached a flight of stairs that twisted around to another flight of much smaller steps, and Thomas came to a stop and switched the flashlight off again. But it wasn't as dark as it had been back in the tunnel, because now there were long windows high up on the walls, throwing the light of streetlamps and the moon down to us.

The buzzing sound was closer now, and I could hear voices too.

Reaching into his coat pocket, Thomas took out four small party poppers in the shape of champagne bottles and handed them to me.

"Only ones I could get," he winked. "Ready? Remember the plan?"

My voice made a squeal instead of a yes as I clutched the party poppers to my chest. Now that we were here, the plan seemed much more scary and impossible than it had in the afternoon.

Signaling to me to press myself as flat as I could against the wall, Thomas led the way toward the two glass doors that opened straight into the main hall. As we approached them, the enormous room beyond came into focus. Black and white floor tiles shone out against the dark like an endless glowing chessboard. They lay under a gigantic golden dome, shaped like an upside-down teacup and held up by a million arches. And right there, directly beneath the dome, in the very middle of a circle of pure white tiles stamped with a spiky star, was a ball of fireworks made of orange and yellow sparks. Just like I had seen at Piccadilly Circus.

But there wasn't just one ball of sparks. There was another . . . and another . . . and another.

There were five thieves! And all of them were dressed in wrinkly black coats and sneakers and had fluffy beards too, and they were trying to break through something in the floor.

"I thought it would just be one," said Thomas, looking confused.

"Five is *too many*," I whispered to Thomas, my voice now shaking almost as much as my hands were. "Let's go back down and call the police," I urged, wishing Mum and Dad didn't think I was still too young to have a cell phone.

"They'll be gone by then," whispered Thomas. "Look, they've already broken through!"

He was right. At that very moment, I heard a loud *PLONK*

followed by lots of groans. The thieves were trying to lift up a huge golden disc cut out from the marble floor. All around its edges was swirly writing, and from its center sparkled the sign of the two swords I had seen on the big black door of the office.

One of the thieves had already started spraying a yellow sign onto the cathedral floor. It looked like a math equation, with the number two standing above a line and a number ten underneath it.

"Trust me," whispered Thomas. "We'll *make* it work, I promise. Just be sure to run as fast as you can, OK? Now we know the alarms are off for sure, it should be easy for you. Let's just hope Catwoman got the message out on time."

And without giving me a chance to say that five thieves might hurt him badly and that I didn't want him to be hurt and that I was scared they might come after me too, Thomas pushed me back around the corner and flung open the doors.

"GOOD EVENING, GENTLEMEN! SO WHAT DO WE HAVE HERE?"

The clamoring of metal and the sound of spraying and groans all stopped. There was a frozen pause, and then a woman's voice shouted back, "WHO IN THE HOLY BLAZES ARE YOU?"

I could hear Thomas's footsteps walking quickly toward the center of the dome.

"I beg your pardon, miss. I'm the man who's being blamed

for your crimes. So I thought I'd just drop by and see what I'm supposed to be stealing this time!"

I shoved the party poppers into my trouser pocket and peered around the edge of the staircase, my insides feeling as if they wanted to be outsides.

This was it. The thieves were all looking at Thomas. This was my chance to sneak into the hall and past them to the front doors and set off the poppers outside so that Catwoman's friends could come and help us catch all the thieves and be our first eyewitnesses and help bring them to the police! All I had to do was *move*!

But I couldn't. Instead, my hands were gripping the walls and my feet were refusing to leave the floor.

I couldn't do it. It was all true, everything that everyone had ever thought about me. I wasn't brave enough. I wasn't good for anything. I was just a menace and a screw-up who couldn't ever do anything right!

The thieves were all starting to surround Thomas, their hands held out in different positions, ready to hurt him.

"Come on, now," Thomas was saying. His voice was calm, but I could tell he was scared. "No need to go after an old man like me. Especially one that you've been taking style tips from."

As one of the bigger thieves lunged and grabbed Thomas by the arms, my whole body lurched forward and my feet suddenly started to move so fast that I couldn't even feel the ground beneath them.

"HEY! YOU LEAVE HIM ALONE, YOU COWARDS!" I cried. As everyone turned to stare at me, I remembered too late that I was meant to have *secretly* run down to the front doors—without anyone seeing! Ignoring the six identically bearded faces all blinking at me, I made my sneakers squeak to the left and began to sprint as fast as I could down the side passage of the cathedral.

"AFTER HIM!" shrieked the woman, instantly causing a flurry of footsteps to echo through the cathedral.

"HECTOR! WATCH OUT!"

I glanced over my shoulder. One of the thieves had already nearly reached me! I swerved to the right and grabbed a table-cloth, pulling it—and the giant candles sitting on it—off the table and letting them clatter to the floor behind me. I heard a loud crash as the thief fell over them and skidded across the floor, crashing into some wooden chairs like a bowling ball.

Cutting across the hall to the middle of the room, where all the long benches were, I saw another two thieves running toward me from the other side of the seats. Like a game of leapfrog, I jumped over the benches, one after the other, as quick as I could. But the corridor was too long and the doors were too far away and it was getting harder and harder to make my legs spring high enough. I could see hymn books lying on some of the seats and cushions, so I grabbed a hand-ful, turned around, and began throwing them at the thieves.

"AAAAAAGH! QUIT THAT, KID!" cried one thief with

an extra-deep voice as I hit him with a book right in the middle of the forehead.

I jumped down from the bench I was on. One thief was moving fast toward me, and I was all out of hymn books! Diving down to the floor, I began feeling for a dropped hymn book or anything else I could throw at him. As I searched the floor with my hands, I realized the benches had gaps between their legs that were big enough to let me roll underneath them. So I dropped to my stomach and rolled back toward where Thomas was being held by two of the thieves, stopping just a few rows away. Holding my breath, I waited for the thieves up ahead to figure out that I wasn't where they thought I was.

"Where is he?" screamed the woman.

"I don't know!"

"Well, check under the benches!" she cried.

Quickly crawling up on to the bench I was under, I lay down flat on top of its long narrow seat and waited silently.

"He's not under here!" shrieked one of the thieves.

As I heard the other two thieves stand up again, I dropped down to the floor and began quietly rolling my way back to the front doors again. But I could hear the footsteps of the thieves pausing every few seconds, which meant they were checking under and over each row on their way down the hall.

"Leave him be!" shouted Thomas. "He's just a kid. He's got nothing to do with any of this."

"Shut it, old man!" screamed the woman as she did something to make Thomas cry out.

I couldn't let them hurt him! I had to distract the thieves again and told my brain to think as quick as it could!

The hymn books . . . they were the only thing I had . . .

Grabbing another book from the bench above me, I slid it along the floor as far as I could, back toward Thomas. After a long moment, there was a loud bang as it hit a bench leg.

"Down here, you nitwits!" cried one of the thieves near Thomas.

The footsteps closest to me began running back toward the dome, passing my row without checking underneath the seat, and leaving me to roll and roll and roll faster than I had ever rolled anywhere before.

Grabbing another hymn book, I slid it across the room. I couldn't see where it went, but it soon crashed into something metal and made a loud ringing noise.

It had hit the base of a huge brass candle holder.

The footsteps of the thieves changed direction, heading to that part of the hall instead as one of them cried out, "Got ya!"

Holding back a laugh, I rolled on again. But just as I was reaching the final row of benches and could see the bottom of the giant doorway I needed to get to, something burst against my leg with a loud *BANG!*

I had accidentally pulled the string of one of the party poppers in the middle of all my rolling, and now my pocket was exploding with streams of paper.

"THE DOORS!" cried three of the thieves all at once. I gave up hiding completely and sprinted as hard as I could toward the doors. Reaching them, I tried to pull open the smaller door just like Thomas had told me to, but it wouldn't move. It was locked! I ran and tried the one next to it, but that was locked too!

"PUSH IT, HECTOR! *PUSH* IT!"

Of course!

Taking a running jump, I pushed against the door and burst out into the cold night air, landing on the top of the main stairs. Waves of colored lights swept over me as the picture on the front of the cathedral changed to a new face. I looked around, expecting to see people waiting to help us— people who Catwoman had summoned—but there was no one there. The streets were as empty and as quiet as when we had left them.

Shoving my hand into my pocket, I frantically pulled out a popper to give the signal—but it was the burst one. I tried again but before my fingers could get to the bottom of the shredded papers, a pair of hands grabbed me by the neck.

"Gotcha," said a deep, gravelly voice.

I wriggled and squirmed, but the grip was too tight.

A taller and much skinnier thief joined us. I saw something shining from his hand. It was a round golden ring covering his smallest finger.

I kicked him in the leg, but it only made him laugh. It was the same laugh I had heard at Piccadilly Circus.

"Well, well, well . . ." Pulling down his fake beard, the man gave me a smile. "Isn't this interesting?"

I frowned. I knew the man's face—and not just because I had seen him at Piccadilly Circus. I had seen him somewhere else too. On the TV . . . in Dad's studio . . . giving a check to a small woman in a bright orange cardigan . . . a woman who worked for a homeless shelter!

"Let's go in and have a little talk with your friend now, shall we?" he said. "I'm sure it will be very enlightening."

"NOT SO FAST!" came a voice as the figure of a woman stepped out from behind the statue of Queen Victoria at the bottom of the stairs.

It was Catwoman!

"Unhand that young man, sir," cried Mason, stepping out from the other side of the statue.

Then, all across the horizon and appearing out of nowhere, as if they had been disguised as the buildings and trees around us, at least ten more men and women who I recognized from Mei-Li's soup kitchen stepped out into the light.

A second later, a flash of blue lit up the street as a police car screeched to a halt next to Catwoman, and Officers Miriam and Philip jumped out.

"GAME'S UP, SIR NESBIT!" shouted Officer Miriam. "NOW DROP THAT BEARD AND COME FORWARD WITH YOUR HANDS UP."

11

The Night Bus Hero's Bench

"WHO'D HAVE THOUGHT IT, EH?" PONDERED CATWOMAN. "SIR NESBIT *and* his daughter, Felicity . . ."

We were sitting on the steps of the cathedral—Catwoman, Thomas, Mason, and me.

"Him a millionaire businessman helping to build homeless shelters, and her a jewel of England! In actual fact, both just thieves. Now I really have seen everything. . . ."

From behind us, we heard scuffling and shouting and turned to see Officer Miriam and Officer Philip pushing Sir Nesbit and his daughter down the steps and toward the awaiting police cars.

"Unhand me! I'm a knight of the realm! A knight! Do you hear me?" cried Sir Nesbit, twisting and turning as if trying to free himself from his handcuffs.

"Yeah, yeah," said Officer Miriam as she pushed him on.

"You'll be the knight of a new realm all too soon, don't you worry about that."

"Shut up, Dad!" said Felicity, trying to give him a kick with her sneakers. Now that I could see her face without a beard, I realized I had seen her too—not on the news, but on the cover of a book that Mum had been reading last year. Something about women and power and indoor strength.

Just as they were about to pass by us, Sir Nesbit flattened his feet against the ground, forcing everyone to stop. Looking down at Thomas, he shouted, "YOU! How dare you mess with the likes of ME! I'll get my revenge on all of you stinking, homeless vermin! You'll see! You can't drive ME out of my city—it's my job to drive YOU all out! I was going to make London truly great again. Not a place so polluted with bums that no one wants to live or work here anymore . . . a place so full of pests like you that half the buildings are practically worthless. MY buildings! But I still OWN this city. And I own the mayor too! You see if Mayor Bainbridge doesn't drive you out yet. His laws are MY laws, and we'll get our way because that's the way of the world! You'll *never* beat us!"

"Shut UP, Dad!" warned Felicity again as she finally managed to land a kick on his shin.

Shaking his head slowly, Thomas stood up. He might have been shorter, and his face might have been hairier and scruffier and older-looking, but it was Thomas who looked like a knight just then. Not Sir Nesbit.

"You listen here," said Thomas quietly as Sir Nesbit wrinkled up his nose in disgust and tried to move away. But Officer Miriam was holding his hands tightly and made him stand still.

"We might not have a knighthood, or even a house for that matter. But at least we don't pretend to be something we aren't. We don't put money before people. And we don't steal from our city to make ourselves richer and more powerful. If anyone resembles a poor, stinking vermin, I'm afraid it's you. Not us. *Sir.*"

Finishing with a smile, Thomas gave a nod to Officer Miriam to show he was done. She gave one back as Sir Nesbit blustered and puffed, and then with a "Come on, sir, let's get you to your new home," she bundled him into a car.

As Felicity followed him, Thomas shook his head again. "What a triple act," he said, looking sad. "Sir Nesbit, his daughter, *and* the mayor. No wonder they could get all the cameras and lights and alarms to stop working. They had the mayor backing them!"

"But if Sir Nesbit hated homeless people so much, how come he donated money to that homeless shelter?" I asked, remembering the news story I'd seen in Dad's studio. "It doesn't make any sense."

"Oh, it makes perfect sense if you look hard enough," said Thomas. "The mayor's new law would have made it illegal for us to sleep on the streets if there was a bed available anywhere—even if that bed happened to be far away from where we usually sleep. By donating money to expand shelters *outside* the city, Sir Nesbit made it so that once that law was passed, we would all have been pushed out to go live in them—far away from our friends and families, and the communities we've made for ourselves. And with us out of his way, he could go right back to hiking up the rental prices on his properties. He would have made ten times the money he had given to those shelters. Kind of like donating a penny to get back a fifty-pound note."

"Disgraceful," said Mason, adjusting his bow tie, which tonight had tiny bowler hats all over it. "Almost makes me want to be an American."

We watched in silence as the police cars containing Sir Nesbit and his daughter, Felicity, and their gang of thieves drove away in a haze of white flashes and blue lights. From all the surrounding streets, people had run out of their doors to get a picture of the thieves being caught, and some of them were even taking pictures of us too. Luckily, the police had put a huge line of yellow tape around the cathedral and put us inside it so that no one could come too close.

"But if Sir Nesbit and his daughter were *already* rich, why would they start stealing things just to get richer?" I asked, still confused. "They had millions and millions of pounds and loads of buildings and things already."

Catwoman shrugged. "Who knows? Maybe no matter

how rich some people get, it's never enough for them. They always want more. And sometimes they become so powerful that hurting other people starts not to matter anymore."

"Hector?"

I looked up at the police officer who was standing on the stairs behind us. "Officer Miriam will be taking you home now."

"Oh no," I whimpered. "I'm going to be in so much trouble." I reached out and grabbed Thomas's arm. "Thomas, can't you come with me? Please? They'll shout less if you come with me."

"All right, son, come on," said Thomas. "Although I don't think they're going to tell you off as much as you think they will."

Thomas was right. When we got home, Mum and Dad and Hercules and Lisa—and even Helen—were all so glad to see me and so excited by everything that me and Thomas had to tell them, that they forgot to tell me off for running away and making them so worried that *they* had called the police too. It seemed my attempts at making a clothes body on the bed hadn't worked: I had left the window wide open so the clothes had blown right across the room and woken everyone up.

"Well, you're a couple of heroes," said Mum.

"Heroes on the night bus!" Hercules said, clapping and looking up at me and Thomas as if we were two large scoops of toffee ice cream.

"Exactly." Mum smiled. "And, Thomas, I really do insist you stay with us tonight. It's the least we can do after you brought our boy home safe."

At first Thomas said no and that he had places to be, but when Hercules clung on to his legs and Helen pulled him to the sofa bed Dad had magically made in his studio, he changed his mind.

The next morning, I got up super early and ran downstairs to see Thomas. I had never had a friend sleep over before and couldn't wait to talk to him about everything that had happened. But when I went into Dad's studio, I saw the bed had been put away and Thomas wasn't there.

I ran into the kitchen. Mum and Dad were in there, laying out the table, but there was still no Thomas. I ran past them to the downstairs bathroom and saw that it was empty too.

He had left us, without even saying goodbye.

"Everything OK, Hector?" asked Dad.

"Do you—do you know where Thomas is?" I asked, telling my throat to stop wobbling like a big fat trifle.

"He said he had some things to take care of," said Mum, putting down some plates. "Why?"

"No reason," I said. Looking up at them, I saw Mum and Dad give each other a quick smile.

They were laughing at me. I couldn't believe it. "It's not funny, you know!" I shouted.

"We never said it was," said Mum, frowning.

"Why do you ALWAYS have to make fun of me? Why do you NEVER care about the things I care about? You're ALWAYS laughing at me and hating on me!" It was as if a dam of words had been unblocked from inside my chest and were all flooding out through my mouth before I could stop them. "And I know you wish I wasn't ever born and that it could just be Helen and Hercules!"

"Hold on there, son," said Dad, putting his hands on my shoulders. "What's going on here? Your mum and I would never make fun of you, and we definitely don't hate you."

"We would never laugh at you," said Mum, reaching out to stroke my cheek. "Whatever makes you think we don't love you every bit as much as your brother and sister?"

I wiped away the wetness around my eyes furiously. I didn't want Mum and Dad to see me crying.

"Oh, honey," said Mum, giving me a hug. "I know we're always lecturing you, but it's only because we know you can do better. You have so many skills and talents, and we get sad thinking that you're wasting them. We just want you to be the kind of wonderful person we know you can be."

Dad nodded and rubbed my arms. "Just look at what you did last night! You were so brave. I'll definitely have to put you and Thomas in my documentary now!"

I looked up at Dad and, for some reason, broke out into a smile. "Really?" I asked, wiping my nose.

Dad grinned. "Absolutely. You did something huge last

night—you revealed the true thieves and saved lots of home-less people from being blamed for something they didn't do. If that's not worth putting into a film, I don't know what is."

"We're so proud of you," said Mum, ruffling my hair and making it messy. "Now, go wash up. I've told Lisa she can come late, so I'm making breakfast canapés!"

I wondered whether, just maybe, I had got everything wrong. Maybe Mum and Dad hadn't always wanted me out of the way like I had thought. Maybe they had just been wait-ing for me to show them that I could be better. And now I knew that I could be . . . I wanted to be. Not just for me. But for Thomas and Mei-Li and Catwoman and Hercules and Randy and Lavinia and anyone else I had hurt.

I would make it up to them. All of them. And I would show them that I wasn't ever going to go back to being the kind of person who made people forget their good memories so much that they ended up feeling homeless.

"I just have to do something first," I said as I quickly ran out of the kitchen. Thundering up the stairs to my room, I changed into some jeans and a T-shirt, grabbed the bus pass, and my skateboard, and ran out of the house.

Rolling through the park, first I headed down to the trees to see if Thomas was back in his old tent. But there was only Sam with the "Forever Young" baseball cap sitting outside it, eating a croissant from a plastic bag. On seeing me he gave me a thumbs-up, but when I asked him if he knew where Thomas was, he just shrugged.

Next, I rolled down to the soup kitchen, but it was too early for it, or the church, to be open, and no one was there, so I headed for the Catwoman's tent behind the station. But she wasn't there either.

"Where is everyone?" I asked out loud.

I skated home quickly to find the whole kitchen table filled with plates of breakfast canapés.

"Come and eat," said Mum. She put five tiny round pieces of toast the size of ten-pence pieces on my plate, each topped with a single mushroom and a spoonful of baked beans. "Now listen, the police rang this morning. We need to take you down to the station in an hour. So once you've finished eating, go put on something that's not your hoodie, and we'll meet you downstairs. Hercules, Helen, you too, please."

"Why have they got to come?" I moaned, looking at Helen.

Mum put on her telling-off face. "Don't make me ground you, please," she said, folding her arms at me. "Not when you've only just become a hero!"

In the car, Hercules kept begging me to tell him more about fighting off the gang of thieves, but I was too busy thinking. I wondered where Thomas was and where Catwoman had got to, and if I would be able to go and see Mei-Li today so I could tell her about everything that had happened and give her back her grandad's bus pass.

As we got nearer to the station, I noticed crowds of people with banners and signs standing along the road, and when we came to a stop outside the front doors, they all began to cheer and wave and clap.

"What's going on?" asked Helen as two police officers pushed everyone back from our car and opened the doors for us.

"This way," said one of the police officers, hurrying us inside so quickly that I couldn't read any of the banners. "The chief inspector would like to have a word."

"About what?" I asked, looking at Mum and Dad, who shrugged their shoulders at me.

Showing us to a huge bright blue wooden door, the police officer knocked on it and, hearing a "Come in," threw it open.

And on the other side, there was Thomas! And Catwoman, and Mei-Li and her dad and grandparents and Mason and Solo and Officer Miriam and Officer Philip, all laughing and waving at us and crying out "Congratulations!"

It turned out that the police had called my mum and dad and Thomas early in the morning before I had woken up, and told them that the chief inspector and the mayor of our neighborhood, Lambeth—not the mayor of London, who had now been arrested!—were both going to present a check for the reward money I hadn't known about.

So on the steps of the police station, that's exactly what they did. They gave us a check that was so big, it took five people to hold it up. And it turned out that all the people with the banners were there for us! Me and Thomas had both become famous. Everyone screamed out Thomas's name and called him their "Night Bus Hero" and called me "Hector the Little Hero" too.

I told them all that Mei-Li had helped by stealing her grandad's senior bus pass for us and, with a grin, gave it back to them. Her grandad shook his head at us both and then held his pass up in the air like a trophy. And Thomas told everyone we would never have figured it all out if it hadn't been for Catwoman.

Because of that, me and Thomas decided to split our halves of the reward money with Catwoman and Mei-Li. Which meant we each got a quarter of fifty thousand pounds—more than any of us had ever even imagined having.

Thomas used his portion of the money to rent a small flat not too far from the park so that he could visit his favorite bench every day and remember his family, and he's started lessons so that he can get his very own bus driving license. Only he doesn't just want to drive a normal bus. He wants one with beds in the back and a little kitchen for hot food and teas so that he can drive across London in the night and help other night riders find a way back off the streets.

Catwoman is using her money to get more help remembering only good things again so that she can be allowed to see her children and her grandchildren for real instead of just through photos. She's also staying in an apartment that's big enough for her and her thirteen adopted cat babies. She says she still misses her tent at times, though, so she sometimes puts one up in the back garden and sleeps in there instead of her new bedroom.

Mei-Li donated half her money to the soup kitchen so that her dad could add more space to it and help feed more people. She's using the other half to give her grandparents an around-the-world trip. But really I think that's so she can sleep in a bedroom on her own for a while. I'm glad the soup kitchen is bigger because there are more people than ever volunteering there now, including me.

As for me, I bought the fastest, baddest skateboard that was ever designed and upgraded my computer games collection. But I still had loads left after that. So I did the three best things I could think of and did them all quickly before I changed my mind.

The first thing I did was ask Mum and Dad and Mei-Li and her dad to help me choose a plaque for Thomas's special bench. We chose a nice, shiny silver one, and got the mayor of our town—not the one who is now in jail for seventeen years—to present it to him as a special thank-you gift from everyone. It doesn't have many words on it, but it's got the most important ones. It says:

> **IN LOVING MEMORY OF LAYLA & MAIA**
> BELOVED WIFE & DAUGHTER OF THOMAS B. CHILVERS,
> OUR NIGHT BUS HERO

The second thing I did was ask Officers Miriam and Philip if they could help me fish Thomas's photo album out of the lake. Which meant telling them that I had accidentally pushed Thomas's trolley into the lake in the first place. After they had stared at me and shaken their heads at the news that there was a whole trolley at the bottom of the park lake, they agreed to help. They got some special divers to go in and try to find it, and they did—along with a lot of other things people had thrown into the lake that they shouldn't have, including old tires and a suitcase full of overdue library books. The album was wet and soggy and some of the pictures needed restoring, so a team of students at a university in the city are helping to dry them and recover them and then fill in anything that's been ruined with extra-expensive computers. That way, Thomas can have them on a file at the university too—just in case anyone else tries to ruin them.

Rescuing the photo album didn't even cost me a penny, and I still had lots of money left over. So the third thing I did was help the soup kitchen and Thomas to buy a new shower van—which is a special van with a shower in the back and boxes of clean clothes—so that it can follow Thomas's night bus around and help homeless people feel clean and fresh too. Dad is going to include it in his new documentary, and Mum said she's going to try and get her environmental charity to help make it fully solar-powered so that the shower water gets heated by the sun instead of a boiler.

But of course, I didn't give ALL of my money away. I'm

not *that* good. Even though Will and Katie now think I've gone over to the dark side and am way too good to be friends with them anymore. I still have loads saved for sweets and chocolates and glitter pens for Hercules. And some extra-strong pimple cream for Helen. Not to mention art supplies so I can draw more comics too. Mrs. Vergara says that since I'm spending more time drawing now than chasing kids in the playground, the school might enter me for that drawing prize next year.

Thomas says I should draw a comic about our adventure and saving all the treasures of London. It won't be like a normal comic book with superheroes who have special powers and stuff. But I think a night bus rider called Thomas, a real-life Catwoman, the biggest teacher's pet on the planet, and a bully-who-isn't-a-bully-anymore might just be cool enough to be heroes too.

Bullies Like Hector

This story features three bullies: Hector, Will, and Katie. Bullies are people who might do some or all of the following:

Name-call or make fun of someone, often for their appearance, race, religious beliefs, gender, or disabilities

Cause physical harm. This can include hitting, pushing, chasing, tripping, or forcefully taking things

Make threats of causing harm

Spread rumors or twist truths

Gang up, outnumber, or harass someone— online or in person

Make a list of all the ways Hector, Will, and Katie bully other people from their school. If you were a friend of someone they were bullying, what might you do? Who could you ask for help?

For more information and resources on how to deal with

the issue of bullying, you can contact the U.S. Department of Health & Human Services (HHS):

HHS.GOV; Toll-Free Call Center at 1-877-696-6775

STOPBULLYING.GOV (managed by the HHS)

Did You Know?

On a single night in January 2019*, 567,715 individuals in the United States were experiencing homelessness, either in emergency shelters, transitional housing, or safe havens. They represent a cross-section of America— every region, family status, gender category, and racial/ ethnic group.

Some organizations working to help the homeless:

The National Coalition for the Homeless
nationalhomeless.org
(202) 462-4822

The National Coalition for the Homeless is a national network of people who are currently experiencing or who

---

* U.S. Department of Housing and Urban Development (HUD) Annual Point-in-Time Count January 2019 have experienced homelessness, activists and advocates, community-based and faith-based service providers, and others committed to a single mission: **To end and prevent homelessness while ensuring the immediate needs of those experiencing homelessness are met and their civil rights are respected and protected.**

National Health Care for the Homeless Council

nhchc.org

(615) 226-2292

The National Health Care for the Homeless Council is the premier national organization working at the nexus of homelessness and health care. Grounded in human rights and social justice, the NHCHC mission is to build an equitable, high-quality health care system through training, research, and advocacy in the movement to end homelessness.

The Homeless Code

This book contains symbols which belong to a real code, the "hobo" code. This code was created so that homeless people (who were once called "hobos") could leave hidden messages on the ground or on buildings telling each other where to find help or how to stay away from danger.

Take a look at the symbols with their real-life meanings below, and guess how each one matches Hector's story.

Chapter Headings

1. Bad water

2. Trolley Stop

3. Be ready to defend yourself

4. Halt!

5. There is nothing to be gained here

6. Authorities here are alert

7. This is NOT a safe place

8. Dangerous neighbourhood

9. The owner is in

10. Kind woman lives here. Tell a sad story

11. An officer of the law lives here

12. There's no use going this way

13. Doubtful

14. Fresh water, safe campsite

15. A kind lady lives here

16. You can camp here

17. Hold your tongue

18. Hit the road

19. This is a well-guarded house

20. Thieves are about

21. The sky is the limit

The Thief's Symbols

◇   Be ready to defend yourself

○   There is nothing to be gained here

///   This is NOT a safe place

⊐   A kind gentleman lives here

▽   Road spoiled. Full of other hobos

◯◯   People and police here frown on hobos

†   Religious talk will get you a meal

$\frac{2}{10}$ Thieves are about

Author's Note

Please always seek guidance from a parent or guardian before approaching anyone sleeping rough with offers of help.

When I was fourteen, I saw an old man with deep-set wrinkles and a fluffy white beard sleeping beside the steps of my local police station. He had a trolley packed high with old bags and newspapers parked beside him and was wearing a long, tattered coat and hole-ridden shoes, suggesting he had been homeless for many years. I saw him again the next day, and the next, always in the same spot at the exact same time. During the weekends, I would sometimes see him looking for food in the trash cans on my high street. He never begged: he simply gathered old bags and newspapers and, if he got lucky, food.

Being painfully shy, I was too scared to speak to him or ask him if I could help in some way. But after a while, he began to notice me. I suppose it must have been strange to see a short, slightly pudgy Asian girl with huge glasses staring at him every day! He began to smile and wave at me—an act that made me instinctively smile or wave back. Shortly after, I began to use my lunch money or save things from my packed lunches so I could leave food with him whenever I saw him.

Sometimes it was a piping-hot portion of fish and chips (a good day!); other times it was nothing more than a squashed packet of snack cakes. I always hoped he would be asleep so that I could leave my small tokens and make a dash for it. But of course he never was, so instead, I would rush up to him, hold out whatever I had, turn bright red and run away as fast as I could!

This went on for a number of years, and I got to understand his patterns. Spring and summer, he slept by the station. Autumn and winter, he would sleep elsewhere—probably somewhere with more cover. But one spring day, as I made my way to college, I noticed the old man wasn't in his usual spot. He wasn't there the next day or the one after that: it was as if he had suddenly disappeared. Along with his trolley.

I finally mustered up enough courage to walk into the police station, and ask if anyone knew where he was. The answer I received cracked my heart: he had died in the night, earlier in the week. His name, as far as the officer knew, had been Thomas. "Just" Thomas.

Thomas didn't know it, but our quiet exchanges had a huge impact on my life. He was a friend—albeit a silent one—and someone I looked forward to seeing every day. After his death, I made a promise to never be too scared or shy to speak to someone in need of help again. So I began working for charities during my summer holidays—starting first with the charity my mum worked for at the time, which built homes for unseen homeless families and women and children fleeing violence.

In the midst of writing this book, a moment in history transpired that led to every single rough sleeper in England being whisked off our streets in under a week and placed in a room of their own. And while this whisking away didn't include the counseling or aid needed to tackle the deep-rooted causes of homelessness, it was proof of one fact: our country has the space to provide the basics.

It took a global pandemic for that space to be identified, but it was done. Proving that every council, rich or poor, can make way and give shelter to its homeless when they feel they need to. The question then has to be: Why isn't that need felt at all times?

Over 700 homeless people died in 2018 in England and Wales. That equates to two homeless people dying every single day. (The figures remain unknown for 2019 and 2020 at the time of this story going to print, but the number is expected to be higher.) And over 320,000 people, including children, are without a home as a result of the traumas life has thrown at them. I hope one day those numbers will hit 0.

In the meantime, this one's for Thomas of East Ham. A friend who was never a "just" to me or the countless others he waved and smiled at.